DEATH IN THE HOLE

Skye Fargo was desperately climbing the ladder out of the desert gold pit when the huge Mohave warrior hit him. The rickety ladder shattered, and Fargo plummeted toward the bottom with the fierce Mohave on top of him.

In midair, the Mohave swung his big war club and clipped Fargo a numbing blow on the shoulder. Fargo twisted to get out from under before they struck the ground.

Then they hit. Stunning agony lanced through Fargo, and the pit was a blur. Dazed, he looked up as the Mohave raised his club for another blow.

The leg irons shackling Fargo made it impossible to dodge. All he could do was launch himself at the warrior's leg. It saved his skull from being smashed, but a moment later the Mohave was astraddle his chest, with the club pressing down on his windpipe. Fargo bucked. He shoved. He tried to butt the warrior in the face. But he could not dislodge the man.

This pit would be the grave of one of them—and from the screaming pain in the Trailsman's windpipe and the grin on the Indian's face, it was clear who the corpse was to be . . .

Be sure to read the other novels in the exciting Trailsman series!

EAGLE

by Don Bendell

Chris Colt didn't believe in the legendary Sasquatch, no matter if witnesses told of a monstrously huge figure who slew victims with hideous strength and vanished like smoke in the air. But now in the wild Sangre de Cristo mountains of Colorado, even Chris Colt, the famed Chief of Scouts, felt a tremor of unease in his trigger finger. The horrifying murderer he was hunting was more brutal than any beast he had ever heard of, and more brilliant than any man he had ever had to best. Colt was facing the ultimate test of his own strength, skill, and savvy against an almost inhuman creature whose lethal lust had turned the vast unspoiled wilderness into an endless killing field. A creature who called himself—Eagle. . . .

from **SIGNET**

*Prices slightly higher in Canada. (0-451-185358—$5.99)

DEATH VALLEY BLOODBATH

by

Jon Sharpe

A SIGNET BOOK

SIGNET
Published by the Penguin Group
Penguin Books USA Inc., 375 Hudson Street,
New York, New York 10014, U.S.A.
Penguin Books Ltd, 27 Wrights Lane,
London W8 5TZ, England
Penguin Books Australia Ltd, Ringwood,
Victoria, Australia
Penguin Books Canada Ltd, 10 Alcorn Avenue,
Toronto, Ontario, Canada M4V 3B2
Penguin Books (N.Z.) Ltd, 182-190 Wairau Road,
Auckland 10, New Zealand

Penguin Books Ltd, Registered Offices:
Harmondsworth, Middlesex, England

First published by Signet, an imprint of Dutton Signet,
a division of Penguin Books USA Inc.

First Printing, June, 1996
10 9 8 7 6 5 4 3 2 1

The first chapter of this book originally appeared in *Washington Warpath*, the one hundred seventy-third volume in this series.

Printed in the United States of America

The Trailsman

Beginnings . . . they bend the tree and they mark the man. Skye Fargo was born when he was eighteen. Terror was his midwife, vengeance his first cry. Killing spawned Skye Fargo, ruthless, cold-blooded murder. Out of the acrid smoke of gunpowder still hanging in the air, he rose, cried out a promise never forgotten.

The Trailsman they began to call him all across the West: searcher, scout, hunter, the man who could see where others only looked, his skills for hire but not his soul, the man who lived each day to the fullest, yet trailed each tomorrow. Skye Fargo, the Trailsman, the seeker who could take the wildness of a land and the wanting of a woman and make them his own.

1861, Death Valley—
a fitting name
for a living hell,
where death was always just
a heartbeat away . . .

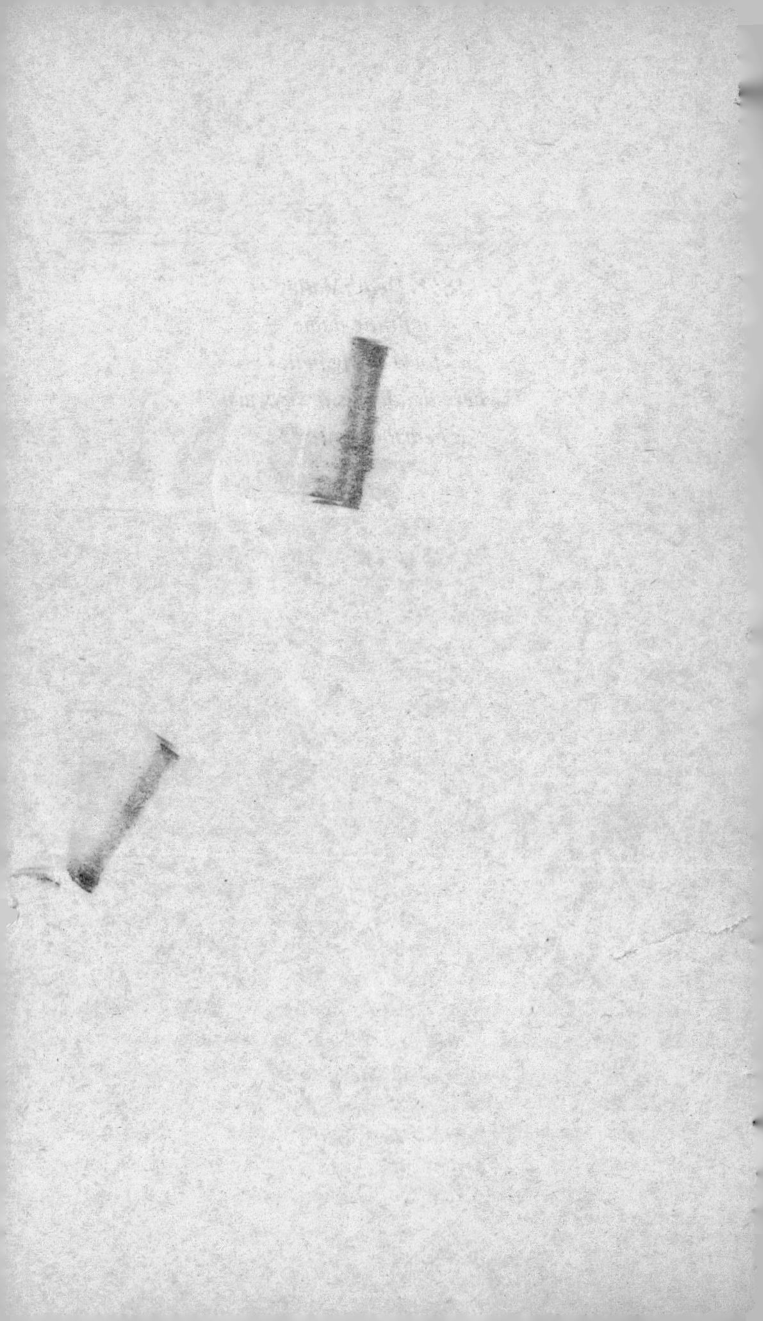

1

Skye Fargo knew the ways of the wilderness better than most men. He had learned many valuable lessons while roaming the West from end to end, and one of the most important had to be that a wise man always rode the high lines when in rough country.

It was plain common sense. Travelers who failed to spot trouble coming paid for their mistake with their lives. Many an unwary rider had fallen prey to hostiles, bad men, or beasts, and Fargo did not intend to be one of them.

On this particular day, the big man with the intense lake-blue eyes was riding northeast from Los Angeles. He intended to follow the Sierra Nevada north to a pass that would take him on into Nevada Territory. It was a trek he had made several times, but even though he knew the lay of the land well, he took no chances. He rode alert at all times, his right hand resting on his thigh within inches of his polished Colt.

A blazing sun had the sky all to itself. Many kinds of colorful birds sang gaily or flitted in the trees. Squirrels and chipmunks frolicked everywhere. On occasion, solitary hawks wheeled high overhead. Less frequently, majestic eagles did the same. Several times since dawn Fargo had spooked deer, and he looked forward to treating himself to a juicy venison steak for supper.

At the sight of a plume of gray smoke, Fargo reined up. So far as he knew, there were no homesteads in that region. Nor were there likely to be anytime soon. Settling there was too risky, since just over the range lay sprawling desert country, home to the fierce Mohave Indians. Wondering if he might have stumbled on a roving band, he rose in the stirrups.

The switchback Fargo was descending wound into a small valley watered by a narrow stream. Someone was down there in a stand of trees on the south bank. Judging by the large amount of smoke, Fargo doubted Indians were to blame. Every frontiersman worthy of the name knew that Indians kept their fires small.

Fargo had no hankering for company. He'd had his share in Los Angeles, having spent a whole week playing poker and dallying with a frisky dove. Besides, he was due in Salt Lake City by the end of the month. So, going on, he came to the valley floor and swung to the right to skirt the stand. He could hear low voices but not distinct words. A horse nickered.

Hugging the tree line, Fargo held the pinto stallion to a walk. He kept one eye on the cottonwoods and spied several figures moving about. When he was almost abreast of them, a glimmer of long blond hair told him a woman was with the group, and he relaxed a bit. Few females rode with outlaw gangs. He cocked his head to see her better, then froze as the metallic rasp of a rifle lever warned him that he had let his curiosity get the better of him.

"Hold up there, mister! And keep those hands where I can see 'em."

To argue invited a bullet. Fargo reluctantly did as the hombre wanted, hiking his arms to show his peaceful intentions. "I'm not looking for trouble," he stressed.

"Who the hell cares?"

The brush parted, revealing a grizzled hard case in buckskins similar to Fargo's, except his were caked with grease and grime from top to bottom. A sparse salt-and-pepper beard covered his lower jaw. He wore a grin belied by the cocked Spencer in his weathered hands.

"I don't like having guns pointed at me," Fargo mentioned calmly enough, given that he wanted to take the Spencer and wrap it around the man's scrawny neck.

"Then maybe you shouldn't go sneakin' around the way you

do," the hard case responded. Moving warily around the front of the stallion, he trained the rifle on Fargo's chest, then tossed back his head and hollered. "Clem! Trench! We got us some company!"

The cry brought a half-dozen others from the stand. Foremost among them was the blonde, a shapely woman who carried herself as if she owned the world. Narrowed green eyes studied the Trailsman as she approached. A riding outfit clothed her lush form, doing ample justice to the enticing swell of her bosom and the inviting sway of her hips. From the neck down she was all soft curves and cleavage, but from the neck up she was as hard as flint. She had a jutting jaw, high cheekbones, and all the warmth of a glacier in her stare.

Beside her stalked a tall man wearing a pair of ivory-handled Colts, slung low. A wide-brimmed black hat crowned a square head perched on broad shoulders. He had big hands; the thumbs were hooked in his black gun belt. His vest, pants, and boots were also black. Large Spanish-style spurs jingled with every step.

"What do we have here, Otis?" the woman said, halting. In her right hand was a thick quirt, which she tapped against her left palm.

"I caught 'im trying' to sneak on by us," the old man declared.

Fargo was taking his measure of the others. They all had the mean look of human vultures, of men who lived by their guns and their brawn.

"Is that true?" the woman asked.

There was no reason for Fargo to answer. He had done nothing wrong and they knew it. Whatever they were up to, they would show their true colors soon enough. His only regret was that he had been harebrained enough to get caught.

The tall gent with fancy hardware stepped forward. "Didn't you hear the lady, friend? She asked you a question. You'll answer her, if you know what's good for you."

Bending, Fargo made a show of examining the man's bull neck.

"What the hell are you doing?"

"Looking for the leash," Fargo responded.

The woman grinned, the man called Otis chuckled, and the tall man in the black hat scowled. Suddenly, brawny hands clamped on Fargo's shirt. He was lifted clear of the saddle and heaved into the grass. Rolling as he hit, Fargo rose into a crouch, ready to defend himself despite the ring of pistols that had blossomed in the hands of the rest.

The blonde moved, smacking her quirt against the tall gunman's chest. "That's enough! And the same goes for all of you! There will be no gunplay unless I give the word. Savvy?"

No one debated the point, so the woman turned and bestowed a smile on Fargo. "Riling Dee Trench isn't the smartest thing in the world to do, mister. He's killed men for a lot less. Once, he shot a gent for looking crosswise at him."

Fargo slowly uncoiled, careful not to lower his hand too near his revolver. The smart thing to do was to go easy, to put a rein on his temper, to hear them out. But he couldn't help himself. "Was the man facing him at the time?"

Trench bristled. His fingers formed into claws. He resembled a bear about to pounce, but at a sharp glance from the woman he held himself in check and slowly let the tension drain away.

"Keep it up, mister," the woman said, "and I won't be responsible for what happens. I'm trying to do you a favor, but you act as if you want to commit suicide."

Fargo nodded at Otis's Spencer. "You call holding a man at gunpoint doing him a favor? Most people would call that being mighty impolite."

The woman walked up to him. Her luxurious hair gave off a minty fragrance that competed with the alluring perfume she favored. Her full lips quirked upward. "Another time and place, and I'd find your sense of humor refreshing. As it is, I'm afraid I have to put business before pleasure." She paused. "What's your name?"

Fargo deliberately stared at her chest. The way her twin peaks pushed against the fabric, it was a miracle she didn't burst from her blouse like an overripe melon. "I don't see any badge," he told her.

Otis snickered. "Uppity cuss, ain't he, Miss Langtree?" He squinted at Fargo. "For your information, mister, we don't need no stinkin' badges. In case you can't count, there's eight of us and only one of you. So you'd best loosen them lips of yours, pronto."

Langtree shushed him with a gesture, then placed her warm hand on Fargo's wrist. "We have no call to snip at each other like this. I'm sure that once you understand, you'll cooperate."

"Don't hold your breath."

Dee Trench took a step, but again the beautiful woman exercised her remarkable control and rooted him in place with a bob of her fine head.

"Now, then," she said, taking gentle hold of Fargo's fingers, "why don't we start this whole business over again, and do it right? I'm Veronica Langtree. I operate a gambling hall in Los Angeles. Perhaps you've heard of it. The Lucky Lady?"

Fargo was impressed. The Lucky Lady had a justly deserved reputation as being the finest establishment of its kind south of San Francisco. Chandeliers, thick burgundy carpet, and mahogany furniture testified to the quality of its clientele. He had visited it once, but the stakes had proven too high for his poke. "You're a long way from home," he commented.

"With good cause," Langtree said. "I'm after a skunk who cheated one of my new dealers out of over ten thousand dollars last week, and I don't aim to rest until he's made good the money."

The story was plausible. Casinos and saloons never tolerated cheats and swindlers, unless they were on the payroll of the house. Professional gamblers knew better than to ply their trade in a first-rate place like the Lucky Lady, where they were more likely to be caught. And more likely to lose a few fingers or teeth as a warning to others.

"He's hiding out in this area?" Fargo asked.

"No, the worm *lives* in this neck of the woods. He's an old prospector by the name of Luke Gantry. Twice a year or so he strays down into Los Angeles to buy supplies and treat himself to a night on the town. This time he just happened to pick my place." Langtree scowled. "He's going to learn the hard way that no one cheats me and lives to brag about it."

It was common knowledge that dealers at joints like the Lucky Lady were the best gamblers in the business. So it seemed strange to Fargo that an ordinary prospector had outwitted one. "You say this Gantry fleeced your man?"

"With one of the oldest tricks in the book. A mirror ring."

Fargo was familiar with the trick. A cardsharp would buy an ordinary finger ring with a flat surface on the band and polish the surface until it gleamed like a mirror. With it, a man could read all the cards being dealt. Plenty of cheats had been hung for using them.

"A friend of Gantry's told on him," the woman went on, and sighed. "I was gone the night Luke stopped by, which is a shame. I would have been suspicious right away. Gantry never won that much money at one time in his whole life. If I'd been there and had him searched, I could have saved myself a lot of trouble."

The blonde sounded sincere, yet at the back of Fargo's mind gnawed a pinprick of doubt. "If you know who you're after, why stop me?" he asked innocently enough, while taking a step to his right, which put him closer to the Ovaro and within arm's length of Otis and that unwavering Spencer. Most of the other gunmen had let their guard down and were not covering him as carefully as they should.

"Because Gantry's shack is too well hidden. We know the general area where to find it, but we could search for a month of Sundays and never hit pay dirt," Langtree said. "He has friends, though, who come out to visit him from time to time. I'm hoping we can persuade one of them to tell us where it is."

Again something did not quite ring true, but Fargo had no time to figure it out.

Trench cut in, snapping, "That someone is you, jackass. Tell us while you have your teeth."

"I don't know any Luke Gantry," Fargo declared. He had to lull them into thinking he had no intention of bucking them, so he smiled, adding, "And it seems to me that you're going about this all wrong. If I were Gantry, I wouldn't hang around. He's probably halfway to St. Louis by now." Another short step put him right where he wanted to be.

Veronica shook her head. "You don't know that old cuss like I do. Gantry will never leave here. He loves it too much."

Otis finally let the barrel of the Spencer dip. Not more than an inch, but it was enough.

The moment Skye Fargo had been waiting for had come. Keeping his tone casual, he remarked, "I haven't seen anyone since I left the coast. Unless you count those Indians this morning."

Every last one of them was intensely interested. Langtree stiffened. "What Indians? Were they Mohaves?"

"I couldn't say," Fargo said, shifting to point to the south. "They were just past that sawtooth ridge on the horizon."

It was one of the oldest ploys around. Fargo hadn't encountered any hostiles. His sole purpose was to distract Langtree and her bunch, to get them to focus on that ridge for a few seconds instead of on him. And it worked better than he had dared hope. Every last one of them turned to study the landmark. The instant they did, Fargo exploded into action. Grabbing the Spencer's muzzle, he wrenched it from Otis's grasp even as he swiveled to slam the stock into the temple of the nearest gun shark. The rifle went off, the slug catching yet another hard case in the shoulder and knocking the man to the ground.

Much too late, Langtree's men realized their mistake. They started to bring up their pistols. Dee Trench went for his, his brawny hands a blur, his draw smooth and graceful, like the striking of twin rattlesnakes. But in this case he was not nearly fast enough.

Skye Fargo only had to pivot to plant a boot in Trench's groin. At the same time, his own Colt cleared leather. It was cocked and extended and touching Veronica Langtree's brow before the others could cover him. "Anyone moves and she dies," he barked.

To a man, they froze. Except for Trench, who had sagged to

his knees with his hands over his manhood and was sputtering and wheezing like a busted bellows, and the wounded gunman, who thrashed on the ground with a palm pressed to his bleeding shoulder.

The blonde, to Fargo's surprise, displayed no fear. She stood there with her chin held high and a hint of a smile curling those luscious lips.

The youngest of her hired help, a thin kid with pimples and a derby, kept glancing back and forth between Fargo and his employer. "You're bluffing, stranger," he said. "You ain't about to shoot a lady in cold blood."

It was Otis who answered. "Crespin! You lower that iron right this second, or so help me, when this is over I'll skin you alive and make you eat your oysters, to boot!"

Veronica spoke. "You heard Otis. I want all of you to do exactly as this gentleman tells you to do. There will be no heroics. Is that understood?"

Fargo seized the advantage while he had it. "Shuck the shells from those cylinders, boys. Then toss the artillery into the grass. And be quick about it."

While they complied, Langtree eyeballed Fargo from head to toe, then commented, "You know, mister, there's more to you than I thought. I haven't met anyone with your kind of grit in a long time."

"You like men who hold guns to your pretty head?"

"I like a real *man*. And it seems they're getting harder to find all the time." Langtree glanced down at Dee Trench. "He tries hard, but he's rough around the edges yet."

Fargo honestly didn't know whether to laugh in her face or feel flattered. He watched her underlings closely, and when the last revolver went flying, he lowered his pistol, holding it pointed at her stomach, just in case. Stepping to Trench, he plucked both expensive Colts from their silver-inlaid holsters and tossed them, then did the same with the wounded gunman's .36-caliber Navy. Wagging his gun, he had Otis, Crespin, and the rest move away from the Ovaro, giving him room to mount.

Trench had stopped sputtering but still was unable to

straighten. Glaring, he growled, "We'll meet again one day, bastard. When we do, I'll make you eat that boot."

"Then you might as well make me eat both, since they're a set," Fargo said. Without warning, he kicked the gunfighter flush in the mouth with his other foot. Trench crumpled, bleeding profusely from a split lower lip.

"Son of a bitch!" one of the men blurted.

Fargo wasn't done yet. Whirling, he strode over to Otis. "As for you, mister," he said, and drove the Colt into the older man's gut, doubling Otis over, "the next time someone tells you they don't like having a rifle pointed at them, maybe you'll listen."

If looks could kill, Fargo would have been blasted to tiny pieces as he backpedaled to the stallion and gripped the saddle horn. Only Veronica Langtree showed no anger or resentment. Oddly enough, her gaze held newfound respect. Fargo hooked a stirrup, then eased into the creaking saddle. "I don't want to see anyone on my back trail."

No one had anything to say.

Lightly applying his spurs, Fargo walked the pinto backward in order to keep Langtree and her hired cutthroats in front of him until he gained the cover of the forest. It was a trick he had taught the stallion long ago, one that had saved his hide time and again. Langtree grinned and waved as the foliage closed around them.

The moment the vegetation screened him, Skye Fargo wheeled his mount and sped at a gallop to the east. His shoulders prickled for over half a mile. He half expected to hear gunfire and see the gunmen hot on his trail. But they never appeared. Only after an hour had gone by was he willing to take it for granted that he had given them the slip.

Fargo was glad to be shy of Veronica Langtree. She was trouble, the kind of person who did as she damn well pleased when she damn well pleased, without any regard for the consequences. If he had to guess, he'd say her beauty hid a heart as cold and calculating as any man's. He had met her kind before and always regretted getting involved with them. No, sir, he reflected. Give him an easygoing saloon girl any day.

The bright sun and abundant wildlife soon took Fargo's mind off the encounter. Presently he spied a long valley to the east, and beyond it the Inyo Mountains. Thanks to the blonde and her men, he had strayed much farther west than he originally intended. It was time to swing to the north again and make for the high pass over the Sierra.

By now Fargo was well up in the high country. He angled across a verdant meadow, scattering butterflies and scaring a pair of grouse into taking wing. Farther on he came to a steep ravine and bore eastward along the rim in search of a trail to the opposite side that would be easy on the Ovaro. Idly, he stretched, and as he did, he happened to glance back the way he had come. Perhaps a quarter of a mile away, sunlight glanced off metal.

Fargo's features hardened. He'd warned Langtree and she hadn't listened, so whatever happened next was on her shoulders. Veering into the pines, he yanked the heavy Henry from its saddle scabbard, worked the lever to feed a .44-caliber round into the chamber, and halted in the shadows. Whoever Langtree had sent was about to learn that trying to bushwhack him was a surefire invitation to an early grave.

It wasn't long before the rider appeared, a stick figure hundreds of yards distant. To Fargo's amazement, the man rode right out in the open, making no attempt at all to conceal himself. Fargo suspected it must be the pimply kid, Crespin. None of the others had struck him as being that stupid.

A minute went by, and Fargo grew puzzled. The rider wasn't sticking to his trail. Instead, the man weaved all over the place, first to the right, then to the left, then straight for a dozen feet before meandering off again. Fargo had no idea what to make of the rider's bizarre antics, unless Crespin had lost the Ovaro's tracks and was hunting for them again. But that couldn't be. The prints were so fresh, a five-year-old could follow them with ease.

Fargo pressed the rifle stock to his right shoulder, took a bead on the rider, and waited for the man's chest to fill the sights. Which didn't happen. The rider appeared to be bent low over the saddle, evidently examining the ground. As the horse drew nearer, Fargo saw that he was mistaken. The man wasn't *bent* low—he hung limply, facedown, both arms dangling, still and lifeless.

Wary of being lured into the gunsights of other men lurking back in the trees, Fargo replaced the Henry and let the sorrel get close to the ravine before he burst from cover. The sorrel nickered and turned to flee, but the stallion was on it before it could. Fargo caught hold of the bridle, bringing the skittish animal to a stop.

The rider had one leg crooked over the saddle horn, the other snagged in a stirrup. It explained why he was still in the saddle. A broad brown hat secured by a chin strap concealed most of his face.

Fargo dismounted. Stroking the sorrel to calm it, he edged to the slumped form. A dark stain high on the man's back framed a bullet hole. Whoever it was had been ambushed, shot from behind. Fargo worked the snagged boot back and forth until it slipped free. Reaching up, he straightened the crooked leg and had to brace himself as the body slid off into his arms. The hat fell, cascading rich black hair across his broad shoulders. At the same instant, he felt large, soft breasts under his forearm. Startled, he found himself nose to nose with an incredibly beautiful woman.

Dark eyes snapped wide. They held a hint of panic, which was promptly replaced by simmering rage. "I'll kill you!" she screeched. Spearing her hands at his face, she clawed at his eyes like a wildcat gone berserk.

2

So swift and unexpected was the woman's attack that Skye Fargo nearly lost an eye. As he jerked his head back, two of her tapered nails gouged into the soft flesh below his left eye and ripped downward, leaving a scarlet furrow in their wake. Before she could strike again, Fargo seized both of her wrists and held on tight.

"You murdering scum!" the woman railed, kicking at his knees.

Fargo danced aside. A glancing blow clipped his right shin, lancing his leg with torment. Sliding his other leg behind hers, he pushed, tripping her. She winced when her back hit, then rammed a knee at his crotch. Twisting, Fargo straddled her and said, "Damn, lady! Calm down! I'm not the one who shot you. I don't mean you any harm."

"Liar!" Her shrill cry wafted on the wind as she strained to heave him off. But her exertions had weakened her terribly. She made one last feeble attempt to dislodge him by whipping her head up to butt him in the jaw, but he was too quick for her.

"Pig!" was her last word before she passed out.

Fargo sat there watching the rhythmic rise and fall of her chest. If anything, she was more amply endowed than Veronica Langtree, and equally as pretty.

Another dark stain marked the exit wound. Fargo unbuttoned the top three buttons on her homespun shirt and peeled the soaked wool back to expose her shoulder. The size of the hole identified the caliber as .44-40 or bigger. It was a fluke she was still alive. A few inches lower or to the left and she would be lying off in the woods somewhere, being feasted on by scavengers.

Fargo needed water to dress the wounds. He recalled a stream about a mile back that would suffice. So, being as gentle as he could, he hoisted her onto his shoulder, toted her to the sorrel, and laid her over the saddle. Using a short length of rope, he tied her securely, then stepped into the Ovaro's stirrups and pointed both animals due south.

Fargo pulled the Henry out and draped it across his thighs. Between the Langtree bunch, the bushwhacker who had shot the woman, and the Mohaves, the Sierra Nevada had become an extremely dangerous place to be. He hugged the heaviest cover, even though it slowed him down. Once, far off, he thought that he heard the ring of a shod hoof on rock. Reining up, he listened for the longest while, but it wasn't repeated.

At last the gurgling stream materialized amid tall pines. In a grassy clearing bordering a gravel bar, Fargo tied the horses and lowered the still unconscious woman. Other than a low groan, she made no sound. He had to spread out his own bedroll, since she had none. For a pillow he folded a heavy blanket.

Starting a fire was child's play. Plenty of dry limbs and brush littered the area. Fargo filled his coffeepot to the brim and set it on to heat up. Meanwhile, he busied himself searching for a long, straight stick about the width of his forefinger. From it he peeled all the bark. Next he slid off her shirt, careful not to jar her or aggravate the wound. Both the entry and exit holes bled lightly.

Once the water boiled, Fargo slid a hand into his right boot and drew his Arkansas toothpick. Razor sharp, it made short work of a square of blanket he could use for a wipe cloth. The water went into a pan. Gingerly dipping the blanket in, he commenced washing the woman's front and back. Knowing women as he did, he covered her breasts first in case she woke up and leaped to the wrong conclusion.

Then came the part Fargo was not looking forward to. He held the stick over the fire until the tip glowed red. Kneeling beside the woman, he gripped her shoulder, rested a knee on her upper arm, inserted the tip into the bullet hole, and ever so slowly pushed. The woman thrashed to life. Her eyes didn't open, but she kicked and heaved and moaned, her eyelids fluttering wildly. A loud hiss arose, along with the odor of charred flesh. Fargo gritted his teeth and did not let up until the hole had been reamed from end to end.

It was the best he could do to stave off infection. Not many people knew it, but more victims of gunshot wounds died of secondary causes than from being shot. Being impaled by an arrow was just as bad, since many tribes daubed the barbed points of their shafts in crude but effective toxins.

A blanket would make a bulky bandage, so Fargo rummaged in her saddlebags. He found two spare shirts, one faded and worn out at the elbows. Rinsing it thoroughly, he cut a half-dozen bandages and spent the better part of a half hour looping them around her shoulder and tying them under her arm. After dressing her in the good shirt, he sat with his back to a log and mulled over what to do.

Fargo was in a bind. He had no desire to linger in the Sierra, yet he couldn't ride off and leave the woman unattended. She wouldn't last three days on her own. Odds were, she would be too weak to forage for food for at least a week. Allow another week for her to regain her full strength, and he was looking at a delay of half a month or better.

Resigned to the cards fate had dealt him, Fargo stripped the horses and tethered them where they could reach the stream and had grass to graze on. The sorrel no longer acted up when he went near it. Its coat, he noticed, was laced with nicks and cuts, indicating the woman had pushed the animal to its limit in order to escape her attacker.

Fargo kept the fire small but erected a lean-to to reflect the heat toward the woman. She was bundled from chin to toe, yet shivered often, her teeth chattering. It was a bad sign.

Dawn confirmed Fargo's fears. A raging fever had developed. Either it would kill the infection, or kill her. The best he could do was dab her with cool cloths and force some soup down her throat.

For forty-eight hours Fargo battled an invisible enemy for

her life. At times she was so still that he thought she had died. At others, she tossed and turned and mumbled in her sleep, her brow slick with perspiration, her clothes drenched. Not until late the second night did the fever break, allowing Fargo to breathe a sigh of relief and catch some sleep. He was so exhausted that the moment he closed his eyes, he was out to the world.

Fargo couldn't say what woke him up. Maybe it was the sensation of being glared at. Maybe it was the rustling of the blanket when the woman lowered onto her side and crawled toward him. Whichever, her outstretched fingers were inches from the butt of his Colt when he snapped awake. Automatically, he clamped a hand on her wrist.

"Is this how you thank me for saving your life? Try to shoot me in my sleep?"

The woman sagged, frowning. Her face was as pale as paper, and she had to lick her full lips a few times before she could speak. "Who do you think you're fooling? The only reason I'm still alive is so you can beat the information out of me."

"What information might that be?"

She snorted and tried to push herself up. "Act innocent all you want to. It won't work. I'm not saying a word. You might as well shoot me right this minute and get it over with."

Fargo rose to slide her onto the blanket. "I hate to disappoint you, lady, but I only kill when someone is trying to kill me. And in your condition, you couldn't harm a flea." He swatted her fingers when she proved him wrong by reaching for the Colt.

"Keep this up," Fargo said, "and you're liable to start bleeding again. You've already lost too much blood as it is. My advice to you is to lie still and mend."

"Go to hell!"

Fargo shrugged. "Suit yourself, lady. But don't say I didn't warn you if you go and make yourself worse." Shaking his head at her antics, he went to the stream and filled the coffeepot. Her eyes followed him every step of the way, a flicker of doubt replacing the blazing hatred that had ruled her so far.

Returning, he filled his tin cup and held it to her lips. "Here. But don't drink too much or it'll make you sick."

The woman obeyed. As he set about making coffee, she studied him closely. "Do you have a name?"

"Ladies first."

"You know who I am. That's why you shot me."

Fargo sighed. "You just can't get it through that thick head of yours, can you? For the last time, I didn't bushwhack you." Sitting by the log, he took a bundle of pemmican from his saddlebags and helped himself to a piece. Her attitude rankled him. After all he had done on her behalf, she insisted on treating him like pond scum. Wistfully, he remarked, "The truth is, lady, if I'd known what a bitch you are, I might have had second thoughts about helping you."

She was startled, and it showed.

"I could have been halfway to Nevada Territory by now," Fargo went on. "Instead, I'm saddled with your rotten company until you're back on your feet."

"You don't believe in mincing words, do you?"

"No."

For the longest while neither of them said a word. Fargo finished the pemmican and leaned back. He heard her clear her throat.

"All right. It's Ava. Are you satisfied?"

"Your parents didn't give you a last name?"

"I'd rather not say."

Fargo shifted. Her dark hair lay plastered thickly to her head. Color was slowly creeping into her cheeks, but she still resembled a living ghost. He revealed his own name, adding, "I have to be in Utah in several weeks, so do me a favor and mend fast."

The day grew overcast. Fargo knew it would rain before sunset, so he moved his belongings into the lean-to, stacking them at the end nearest Ava's feet. She observed everything he did, tensing whenever he passed close to her. The last item stored, he grabbed the Henry and stood. "I'll be back as soon as I can."

"Where are you going?" she asked nervously.

"Hunting. You need to get some solid food in you." Fargo turned to depart, then hesitated. There were grizzlies in the Sierra. There were mountain lions. And human vultures who wouldn't hesitate to take advantage of a helpless young woman. Against his better judgment, he drew the Colt and faced her.

Ava saw the pistol. She recoiled, exclaiming, "Oh, God! I knew it!"

Reversing his grip, Fargo held the revolver out. "Take this. You need to be able to protect yourself. I won't go that far. If I hear a shot, I'll come running." He was taking a risk, but he didn't see where he had any choice. In her frazzled state, she might blast away for no reason at all, or shoot him in the back as he crossed the clearing.

Ava could not seem to believe her eyes. She glanced at him, and at the pistol. Then, as if afraid he would change his mind, she snatched the Colt, clasping it to her chest. Her thumb curled around the hammer.

As Fargo started to go, the hammer clicked back. He looked down into the barrel of his own six-shooter. Ava's features were flushed and set in grim determination. She was so weak that she could barely hold the heavy revolver steady, but she managed. He waited, ready to swat the barrel aside if she moved her thumb off the hammer. Sweat broke out on her forehead. She gnawed on her lower lip. Tiring of her foolishness, he snapped, "If you're going to do it, do it. I don't have all day."

The woman uttered a low whine, jerked the gun down, and closed her eyes. "I can't," she said softly, more to herself than to him. "I'm not a cold-blooded killer."

"That makes two of us."

Her eyes shot open again as Fargo walked off. Fording the stream at the gravel bar, he roved along the opposite bank, seeking fresh sign. Here and there he came on deer tracks, but none that had been made recently. At one point a fallen tree had formed a shallow pool, and as he swung to the right to skirt it, he set eyes on a print at the edge of a strip of mud. It was a moccasin track.

Fargo hunkered down to examine it. Based on how dry it was and the amount of windblown bits of grass and leaves littering the bottom, he guessed that the print had been made two weeks ago, possibly longer. Any traces of stitching had long since been obliterated, so he couldn't identify the tribe.

One fact was clear, though. The warrior had not been a Mohave, since they all went barefoot. They were a desert people, who only came into the mountains to hunt game or to raid enemies. Warfare was part and parcel of their way of life, which explained why their arid domain was shunned by other Indians and whites alike.

Fargo did not judge the print cause for concern. It had plainly been a lone hunter, not a member of a larger war party. He resumed his own hunt. Shortly before noon he located a trail made by several deer that had come down to the stream to drink that morning and then gone into thick brush on a nearby slope. Fargo tracked them, avoiding twigs that might snap and give him away.

The deer had bedded down in a thicket. Among them was a young buck. At a range of seventy yards, Fargo sighed and fired. The buck flipped over, kicked once, and was still. It took over an hour to skin the animal, carve off as much meat as he could carry, and wrap it in the hide.

Ava was no longer flat on her back when Fargo returned. She had propped herself against the lean-to, the Colt in her lap, and was sipping coffee.

Fargo had to admire her sand. She was as tough as they came. Most people would have been too weak to move, let alone make do for themselves as she was doing. It gave him hope that she would be on her feet much sooner than he had counted on.

Placing the bundle by the fire, Fargo unfolded the hide. He carved a big steak for himself and a smaller portion for her, and set them aside for later. Venturing into the forest, he selected an armful of long limbs. These served as the frame for the drying rack he fashioned. The woman watched him but made no comment until he started to slice the remainder of the meat into thin slices.

"I've been doing some thinking, mister. I have something to say to you, but it's hard for me to do."

Fargo went on slicing.

"Aren't you listening? I want to apologize for the way I've treated you."

"You should."

Ava made a sound reminiscent of an irate chipmunk. "You can be awful exasperating, you know that? There's no need to rub my nose in it. I thought you were one of those who were after me. Plainly, I was wrong. I'm sorry."

"Why would anyone want to kill you?" Fargo inquired.

The woman had a habit of biting her lower lip when she was disturbed, and she did so now. "I'd like to tell you. I really would. But my pa would have a fit. He doesn't cotton to outsiders much. Our problems are our own, he says."

"Was he with you when you were shot?" Fargo asked, while draping a strip of venison over the rack.

"No, I was hunting by myself. Either me or one of my sisters has to come up here from time to time after game. There's not much to live off of down in the desert country, unless you count all the crawling critters." She took a sip of water. "None of us are very fond of lizard and snake meat, except Pa, of course. He'll eat anything. Even bugs if he has to."

Fargo, his curiosity piqued, went on cutting the deer meat. He knew that if he questioned her, she would refuse to answer. To learn more, he had to act as if he were not really interested. So he commented, "You wouldn't catch me living there. I've been through deserts before. It gets hot enough to roast a man alive."

"It's rough, I'll admit," Ava said. "But the Indians have been living there for more years than anyone can count, and they get by quite well." She stared into the cup. "It's not so bad if you lay low during the afternoon, when the heat is the worst. We do most of our work at night, anyway."

"What kind of work?" Fargo made the mistake of asking. She fell silent, unwilling to answer. In due course he finished laying out the meat to dry. He had positioned the rack under an overhanging tree in anticipation of the rain, which began toward the middle of the afternoon. A light drizzle pattered the ground at first, growing heavier as time went by.

Fargo stretched out in the lean-to with his head propped in his hands. He ignored Ava, who acted as if she wanted to say something but never quite mustered the courage. To the west, lightning crackled. Booming thunder echoed off the peaks. A dank scent filled the air. The sorrel pricked its ears and pranced nervously at the end of the picket rope. Fargo was ready in case it attempted to bolt.

Ava dozed off. In repose, her face was the face of a sensual angel, smooth and soft and inviting. Her cherry-red lips were slightly parted.

Fargo wondered what sort of man would drag his daughters off to live in the desert, and why. There was much more to the whole affair than she was letting on, but she had made it clear that she did not want him prying.

The storm increased in intensity. Lightning flared frequently, while the rumble of thunder was nearly continuous. A downpour bent the trees and roiled the surface of the stream.

Fatigue nipped at Fargo. He started to doze off and rolled onto his side, facing the forest. Yawning, he saw large drops splattering the meat rack. Suddenly something took shape beyond it. For a few brief moments the rain slackened. The sheet of water parted, revealing a dark figure on horseback. Fargo shoved into a crouch, but the rain picked up again, obscuring the rider.

The Henry in hand, Fargo moved to the end of the lean-to to scour the woods. The downpour thwarted him. He couldn't see to the edge of the clearing, let alone into the trees. He had no way of knowing if the person had spotted him, and if so, no way of predicting whether the rider would turn out to be friendly, or a foe.

The thunderstorm lasted another fifteen to twenty minutes. Gradually the rain tapered to a drizzle again. Fargo was not surprised to see that the horseman was gone. Pulling his hat brim low, he darted into the vegetation and made for the spot where he believed the rider had been. There were no tracks to confirm it. The heavy rain had washed away every print.

Fargo made a circuit of the camp to be on the safe side. As he reentered the clearing, Ava sat up. When she saw that he was no longer in the lean-to, she looked all around. On spotting him, she smiled and eased back down.

"There you are. I thought maybe you got tired of my company and left me on my own."

Fargo strode up to her and reclaimed his Colt from her lap. He flipped open the loading gate, checked the cylinder, then shoved the six-gun into his holster.

"Is something wrong?"

"I saw someone," Fargo revealed. "It might have been one of the hard cases I tangled with a few days ago." Briefly, he told her about Veronica Langtree's outfit. She listened intently. "I figured that I gave them the slip," he concluded, "but they've had more than enough time to catch up. There was an old man with them who might be a fair hand at tracking."

"Otis," Ava said.

Fargo looked at her. "You know them?"

She nodded. "Who do you think shot me?"

A dozen questions were on the tip of Fargo's tongue, but just then the sorrel lifted its head, peered off into the pines, and whinnied. In three bounds he reached the animal and wrapped a hand around its muzzle to keep it quiet. But the harm had already been done. From off in the woods came an answering nicker.

"Keep low," Fargo whispered to Ava, and sprinted into the vegetation. His aim was to intercept the rider before the man reached the clearing. The crack of a twig enabled him to pinpoint the approaching horse. Spotting a dusky shape, he ducked behind a tree trunk. The animal advanced slowly. He could not get a good look at it until it stepped into an open space less than thirty feet off, and when he did, he cursed under his breath.

No one was in the saddle.

To the south, another horse neighed. Which meant there were more than one of them. Maybe a lot more.

Pivoting, Fargo raced toward the clearing. He wanted to kick himself for leaving Ava unprotected. If it were Langtree and her men, they might gun Ava down before he could get there. But no shots shattered the stillness. Crashing through a wall of high weeds, he halted at the sight of the empty lean-to. They had gotten Ava.

Movement in the undergrowth on the other side of the stream galvanized Fargo into plunging across. He churned up the bank, barreled into the trees, then paused to get his bearings.

To the southwest, propped against a bole with her head bowed, was Ava. Fargo ran to her, every nerve jangling. No one appeared, so he dipped onto his left knee and gripped her by the chin. "Can you hear me?" he whispered, giving her good shoulder a light shake.

Ava looked up. "You should be more worried about yourself than about me." She paused, then added earnestly, "I'm sorry. I truly am."

Fargo did not need to ask why. Behind him something rustled. He spun, but she had distracted him just long enough. A shadow swooped toward his head and exquisite pain exploded within his skull. He slumped as a larger shadow swallowed him whole.

The last sensation Fargo felt was his forehead smacking the dank earth.

3

Skye Fargo revived slowly, struggling up from a bottomless pit. He would grow dimly conscious of a swaying movement, then slip into darkness again. About the fourth or fifth time, he came awake and stayed awake. His head pounded. His stomach was queasy. Someone had thrown him belly down over the Ovaro and looped rope between his wrists and his ankles. He tried to move but could not.

Twisting his head, Fargo saw stars sparkling in the firmament. An inky silhouette was all he could see of the rider leading the stallion. Behind him rode someone else. When they rounded a bend, a third horseman was visible.

Fargo resigned himself to the inevitable. Presently a tinge of pink framed the eastern horizon, indicating dawn was not far off. Apparently, they had been riding all night long. He noted the position of the Big Dipper and the North Star, which revealed they were bearing to the southeast.

Sunrise was spectacular. Vivid streaks of red and orange decorated the sky, blending into the deep blue of daytime. A few gray clouds were all that remained of the storm that had passed through the day before.

Fargo thought that his captors would stop, but they pressed on. He craned his neck for a glimpse of them. In front of the pinto rode a lean figure wearing a faded shirt, a vest, and jeans. A tilted black hat concealed the person's head.

As they climbed to a low ridge, Fargo saw the one behind him clearly. He shouldn't have been surprised, yet he was. It was a woman, a slightly more mature version of Ava, her face showing a strong family resemblance but her mane of hair reddish instead of black. He caught her eye and declared, "There's no need for this. You can turn me loose."

At the sound of his voice, the lead rider wheeled around. It was another woman, maybe a year or two older than the second, maybe five years older than Ava. Her raven locks had been clipped short, above the shoulder. Her body boasted more angles than curves, but she was still exceptionally attractive. Coming back alongside the stallion, she drew rein.

"Howdy, mister. I didn't reckon you would recover so soon. Usually when I wallop someone, they stay out for a day or better."

"That was you? What did you use, a tree limb?"

"A rock." She smiled. "A big rock."

"I'm not your enemy," Fargo told her. "Just ask your sister, if you haven't already."

The woman's mouth pinched together. "You know we're kin, do you?"

"Ava mentioned you." Fargo nodded at his wrists. "Cut me loose and I'll be on my way. We can forget any of this ever happened."

"Sorry, mister," she responded. "Pa is the one who has to decide what's to be done with you. In the meantime, you'll just have to bear with us." Bending, she gripped his jaw and turned his head from side to side, admiring his profile. "Between you and me, I hope he lets you live. You're about as handsome a man as I've run across." She grinned. "My name is Willa, by the way. That redhead yonder is Dorette."

"Where's Ava?" Fargo asked in the hope that she would speak in his defense and persuade her sisters to let him go. He should have known it would not be that easy.

Dorette overheard and tugged on a lead rope she held. The sorrel clumped up next to her. On it, doubled over, barely hanging on, was Ava. She raised her head, smiled feebly at him, then slumped again.

"Are you trying to kill her?" Fargo bluntly asked Willa. "Your sister needs rest. Lots of it. Keep pushing her the way you are and she's liable to die."

"You reckon I don't know that?" Willa frowned. "It just

can't be helped. The same ones who shot her are out for our blood, as well. Ava will get all the rest she needs once we're safe."

Fargo's face was swished by her mount's tail as she turned it. "Where are you taking me?" he demanded. "At least tell me that much."

"Sorry, handsome. It's our little surprise."

They rode on. The day grew steadily worse, with Fargo enduring hour after hour of grueling torture. His insides were jarred and bounced about to where he swore his stomach must be black and blue. His wrists and ankles became chafed, his right wrist so severely that the rope bit into the flesh, drawing blood. He suffered bouts of being light-headed. And to compound his misery, as the day waned, the temperature climbed. They descended to a valley where it had to be ninety-five or better, crossed to another range, and climbed a game trail to a notch between two mountains.

But then the sun perched on the western horizon. Fargo was confident the sisters would finally call a halt, but to his annoyance, they gave no such sign. It dawned on him that the women intended to push on until they reached their destination.

Exactly where they lay did not make itself apparent until shortly before sunrise. Fargo had dozed off several times during the long, arduous night, and in each instance he had been jolted from slumber by the movement of the Ovaro. He had the impression of climbing, of wind whipping his hair at the summit of another range, and of descending a series of steep slopes. About an hour remained of night when they stopped to rest the animals on a narrow shelf. At first Fargo could not see much of the surrounding countryside. As the light increased, he discovered what appeared to be an enormous arid trough below. It stretched for as far as the eye could see to the north and the south. From five to fifteen miles wide, it was as blank a landscape as any Fargo had ever seen.

Willa had dismounted. She now strolled over and leaned on the stallion. "Figure out where you are yet, handsome?"

Fargo was about to say that he had no idea, when the truth

hit him like a bolt out of the blue. He scanned the baked expanse of desert and licked his dry lips. "You're loco if you're going down there. That's Death Valley."

Willa nodded. "And that's where our pa is."

The valley had gotten its name after a foolhardy band of pioneers barely made it across some years before. It was common knowledge that no one in their right mind entered Death Valley unless they had a hankering to meet their Maker. Not only was it one of the hottest spots in all of North America, but there were virtually no water holes, fierce Mohaves roamed it at will, and rattlesnakes and Gila monsters were as thick as fleas on an old coon dog.

Below the shelf lay a small spring where Willa and Dorette filled water skins they carried. From there Willa wound down a narrow path to the base of the mountains and struck out directly across the parched terrain. Soon the air became as hot as an oven.

Fargo broke out in a heavy sweat. Drops trickled down his face into his eyes, stinging them. The higher the sun climbed, the more stifling it became. The four horses plodded along, on the brink of exhaustion. He doubted whether any of them would last to reach the other side.

The peaks were a mile to the rear when Willa abruptly changed direction, heading south. From her saddlebags she took a small telescope and surveyed their back trail.

Dorette, who had yet to speak one word to Fargo, drew her horse up next to Willa's. For a while the pair conversed in hushed tones.

Fargo had a chance to see Ava up close, and he did not like what he saw. She clutched the saddle horn with both hands and had resorted to the trick of sliding her small feet through the stirrups to keep from falling off. Her cheek rested on her mount's slicked neck. She was deathly pale once more. Ragged breaths passed her gritted teeth, the perspiration caked her face. Unless they stopped soon, she would not make it through the day. He called Willa's name and pointed the fact out to her.

The woman snickered. "It's real sweet of you to be so worried about little sister, handsome. But don't fret. We know what we're doing. And she's a damn sight tougher than you give her credit for being. We all are." She raised the telescope. "We can thank our pa for that. Since the day we were born, he's been hauling us all over creation, through the most god-forsaken country you can think of. We've had to learn to be as hard as the land itself. Savvy?"

It was no secret that hardship either made people stronger, or broke them. Fargo understood, and said so, adding, "Why didn't your father ever settle down and give you a proper home? Wouldn't your mother stand up to him?"

Willa's features clouded. "Our ma died giving birth to Ava. We've had to fend for ourselves ever since. Now hush. It's too damned hot to be chattering like squirrels."

Fargo couldn't dispute that. If he had to make a guess, he would say the temperature had climbed to one hundred and ten, if not higher. His body felt as if it were a sponge being wrung dry of every last drop of moisture it contained.

The blistering ride seemed to take forever, but Fargo knew they had only gone about five miles when Willa reined up, stood in the stirrups, and scoured the parched land they had covered with her spyglass one last time. Satisfied, she smirked and replaced the telescope in her saddlebags. "Well, Dorette, I reckon we gave that bitch the slip."

The redhead nodded, then adjusted a blue bandanna she always wore around her neck.

Fargo was dying for some water. "Isn't it time we all had a drink?" he suggested.

"Be patient, big man. It won't be long," Willa replied.

They traveled another mile to the north. Then Willa slanted to the east, toward the Amargosa Range. Fargo tried to note peaks and other landmarks ahead but he soon wearied of holding his sore neck high enough to see the mountains clearly. The blow to his head and two days without food and water had taken their toll. There were limits even to his superb endurance.

Willa and Dorette knew right where they were going. They crossed Death Valley at one of its narrowest points, entering a gully at the base of the mountains that broadened into a wide gorge, where the clatter of their animals' hooves rang off the high walls. Those walls also reflected the blazing heat of the sun, making Fargo hotter than ever.

Just when Fargo thought he would pass out, they rounded a bend. Fifty yards beyond, the gorge ended at a steep cliff. At its base crackled a small campfire. To the right, four burros were tethered. Blankets, saddlebags, shovels, picks, and other supplies were scattered close to the fire.

Suddenly, dirt and dust spewed up from out of the ground close to the cliff. For a moment Fargo thought he had imagined it. He blinked the sweat from his eyes to see better, just as more earth sprayed into the air.

The women drew rein. Willa slid from the saddle, cupped a hand to her mouth, and bellowed, "Pa! We're back! Get your carcass up here! Sissy's been hurt!"

The dirt stopped flying. Someone muttered in a gravelly voice, and shortly a head poked into view. A tousled tangle of dirty brown hair framed a square face blanketed by a bushy beard that hung halfway to the man's waist. Dark eyes fixed on Fargo. "Who the hell is that?"

"Company," Willa said. "Come over here and show you have some manners."

Their father stomped up out of the hole, or whatever he was in, and barreled down the short incline. "What the hell has gotten into you idiots? That last one gave us no end of trouble, and now you drag back another stray? Didn't I tell you that we'd be better off doing it all ourselves from here on out? Why don't you girls ever listen to me?" The man was red in the face from his outburst. Baggy clothes dotted with holes covered his stocky frame. Dust coated him from head to toe. Ignoring Ava, he seized Fargo's jaw and twisted so he could study Fargo's face. "I don't like the looks of this varmint. You can tell he's tougher than most. Kill him."

Willa and Dorette exchanged glances.

"What are you waitin' for?" their father demanded. "Drag him off somewhere, blow his brains out, and get back here pronto so you can take turns diggin'. I've had to do all the work while you gals were off gallivantin', and I could use some rest."

Neither Willa nor Dorette moved.

"Didn't you hear me? Get crackin'."

"No," Willa said.

"Are you talkin' back to me, girl? I won't stand for any sass."

Willa stood firm. "It wouldn't be right to make wolf meat of the man, Pa, not after he helped sissy the way he did. She was back-shot. We both know by who. If not for Fargo, here, she would have been a goner."

"Fargo, is it?" The man glanced at Skye. "Well, mister, I'm grateful for what you did for my baby. Another time, another place, I'd treat you to a drink and let you stay a spell. But we can't have anyone knowin' where the diggins are." He jabbed a dirty finger at Willa. "Use my shotgun. That way he won't suffer much."

"Haven't you heard a word I've said?" Willa responded. "We don't want him shot. And that's final."

"Oh, it is, is it?" their father countered angrily. His right hand rose from his side, holding a bowie knife. "Fine. Be that way. I'll slit his throat right here and now and be done with it."

Fargo winced as his hair was gripped by steely fingers. His head was wrenched to one side, exposing his throat. He attempted to pull loose but it was impossible. Cold steel touched his skin and he braced for the killing stroke.

"Sorry about this, mister," the father said. "But a man has to do what's best for his brood. If it's any consolation, we'll say a few words from the Good Book over your grave. Do you proper."

Death loomed for Fargo, and he was powerless to prevent it. He saw the man's arm muscles tense.

Suddenly, slender fingers fell on the hand that held the knife. Dorette shook her head, saying softly, "No, Pa."

"Damn it. Don't interfere," the man groused.

"No."

For tense moments, a mental tug-of-war took place, Dorette refusing to back down and her father refusing to listen to reason. Then the man growled like an irate bobcat and snapped his arm down.

"Damn it all! It's a fine state of affairs when a man's own kin turn against him!" Sliding the knife into its sheath, the father stomped off, muttering again.

Willa came over to the stallion and patted Fargo on the head. "You're lucky Pa has had a soft spot for Dorette ever since those Mohaves got ahold of her. It's the guilt, I suppose. He can't hardly refuse her a thing anymore."

Fargo was too worn out to ask what she meant. He would have liked to thank the redhead, but she had already turned away. Moistening his mouth, he said, "I've put up with all of this I'm going to. Cut me down—now. Or so help me, there will be hell to pay if I ever get loose on my own."

"Whatever you want, handsome," Willa teased. From under her vest she slipped a knife. *His* Arkansas toothpick. "Nice blade you've got here," she commented. "We'd never have known you had it if Ava hadn't told us."

Fargo's circulation had been cut off for so long that when the ropes were slashed, try as he might, he could not move his arms or legs. Willa noticed, propped a shoulder under his, and pushed. She'd only meant to boost him from the saddle, but wound up dumping him flat on his back. The back of his skull cracked hard, and for a while the sky and the gorge walls spun around and around. When his senses calmed, a painful tingling crept down his limbs, growing worse and worse with each passing moment. He tried to wriggle his fingers and toes but they refused to move. The anguish mounted. He gritted his teeth, telling himself that it would subside in time, that all he had to do was be patient. It proved to be easier thought than done. It felt as if a thousand red-hot needles were being plunged into him.

There was a commotion close by. Fargo saw Willa and Dorette easing Ava from the sorrel. Their father was nowhere to be seen, which suited him just fine. That old man struck him as being as cantankerous as a rattler and twice as dangerous.

Still the pain climbed. His wrists pulsed with agony. The tingling spread down his fingers and toes. To hasten his recovery, Fargo forced them to bend. It was difficult at first, requiring all the willpower he could muster. Once he succeeded, the tingling began to taper off, the pain to lessen. He plugged away until he could raise his arms and bend his legs.

Willa's face materialized above his. "How are you doing, handsome? We're fixing to have some grub. Care to join us?"

"You need to ask?" Fargo snapped.

"My, aren't we grumpy. Here I thought you'd be tickled pink that you're going to live. Some folks just don't know when they're well off." Sniffing, she flounced toward the cliff.

Fargo began to wonder if maybe the whole family had spent too much time under a hot sun for their own good. He remembered stumbling on a man once down Santa Fe way who had lost his horse and been forced to cover over fifty miles on foot to reach the nearest town. It had been August, the worst month of the year. When Fargo found him, the man had been slinking along like a snake, spouting gibberish, every square inch of skin blistered and cracked. A doctor had declared it to be hopeless. The sun had fried the man's brain.

With an effort, Fargo sat up. The father was over by a pile of provisions, rummaging through packs in search of something. Ava had been placed near the fire and propped on a saddle. Dorette was mopping her face with a damp cloth. Willa busily fixed their meal.

Fargo had to try twice before he could stand. His first awkward step nearly pitched him onto his face. Recovering, he shuffled toward the fire, gaining strength as he went. The father gave him a nasty look but made no move to interfere. Which was just as well for him. Fargo was in no mood to tolerate any more of their nonsense. He was going to eat, rest a spell, and ride on out of there, and no one had better try to stop him.

As Fargo passed the Ovaro, he saw the brim of his hat sticking out from one of his saddlebags. Someone had crumpled the hat up and stuffed it in. His annoyance growing, he retrieved it, slapped the crown and brim into shape, and jammed it down on his head.

"Well, look at you! Up and about so soon!" Willa declared, while stirring stew in a large pot.

Fargo stood over her and balled his fists. "I want my Colt, my Henry, and my knife, and I want them now."

Willa did not stop swirling the big spoon. "Listen to you! Typical man. I'm supposed to drop everything and wait on you hand and foot." She wagged a finger at him in reproach. "Well, in case you haven't noticed, my little sister is about ready to give up the ghost. If we don't get some food into her, and fast, she's a goner."

There was no denying that, but Fargo still wanted to get his hands on his hardware.

"Just hold onto your britches for a few minutes and I'll fetch them," Willa added. "If you can't wait that long, your pistol and that shiny rifle are on Dorette's horse, rolled up in her bedroll. As for your blade—" She produced the toothpick with a flourish.

Fargo squatted and slid his knife into the thin sheath attached to his right ankle. He started to rise, but a spasm in his right calf stopped him.

"You'd better go easy for a while, handsome," Willa advised. "Your muscles have to be worked some before you'll be up to snuff again. Exercise and rest, that's what you need."

"What I need," Fargo said, "is to get the hell out of here. I'm leaving as soon as I collect my things."

Willa acted hurt. "You make it sound as if you don't much care for our company."

"Lady, you nearly split my skull with a rock. You trussed me up like a turkey, hauled me over two mountain ranges and across Death Valley, and didn't see fit to give me a drop to drink the whole time. And now you have the gall to wonder why I'm not all that fond of your company?" Fargo shook his head in disbelief.

"It's not right that you should hold a grudge over a few minor inconveniences," Willa said sternly. "It's not as if we were out to harm you. We've been right friendly, if you ask me."

The cramp in Fargo's calf was growing worse instead of

better. Sitting, he stretched both legs out, which relieved the discomfort a little. Dorette was watching him closely. When he looked at her and smiled, she blushed and averted her gaze.

The oldest sister laughed. "She's always been a mite shy, handsome. A man so much as says hello to her and she about keels over in fright." Picking up a wooden bowl, she began ladling it full of stew. "How about a bite before you go? It's the least we can do after the hard time you claim we gave you."

A tiny voice at the back of Fargo's mind warned him to refuse, warned him to get up and get out of there. But his rumbling stomach overrode it. His mouth watered in anticipation of savoring the thick broth and big chunks of meat. "It can't hurt," he said gruffly.

Willa generously filled it to the brim. Smiling sweetly, she leaned toward him, offering the bowl. Fargo bent to accept. Then suddenly, taking him completely by surprise, she hurled the contents into his face. The hot broth got into his eyes and mouth and splashed up his nose. He instinctively brought his hands up and jerked backward. As he did, something heavy struck him in the chest, knocking him flat. There was pressure on his ankles, followed by a pair of loud clicks. Sputtering and spitting, Fargo cleared his vision and went to stand. Only he couldn't.

His ankles were clamped in leg irons.

4

For a few seconds Skye Fargo was too flabbergasted to do more than gape at the rusty shackles that encased his legs. Then raw fury coursed through him and he glanced up to find Willa and her father standing above him, chuckling smugly to themselves at the clever trick they had pulled.

It was the last straw. Fargo had put up with a lot from the women, more than he would have tolerated from anyone else, in the belief that they were only doing what they thought was necessary to protect themselves from someone who might be out to harm them. He had given them the benefit of the doubt—and they had literally thrown it back in his face.

Now Fargo surged up off the ground and lunged. Willa skipped out of the way, but her father was a hair too slow. Fargo caught hold of the man's arm, spun him around, and planted a fist in his gut that doubled him over. A left hook jackknifed the father backward. Fargo went to take a step, but the leg irons brought him up short. He tripped and fell. In doing so, he contrived to throw out his hands and grab the father. They tumbled together, Fargo on top. He smashed a left fist to the man's cheek, a right to the jaw, and was drawing back his arm for yet another blow when the barrel of a rifle was shoved against his temple.

"That's enough, handsome, unless you want your brains splattered all over your shirt!"

Fargo made no sudden moves. He was breathing much more heavily than he should, thanks to his fatigue and lack of nourishment. Willa stepped around in front of him, motioning for him to get off her father. He obeyed, sliding onto his knees.

"You shouldn't have done that," she said.

Her father rose slowly, wiping at a smear of blood on his lower lip. "That's quite a punch you pack there, mister. You're a strong one. Which is nice to know. It means you'll save us a heap of work."

It was all Fargo could do to keep from tearing into the bearded lunatic again, even with the gun covering him. "What the hell are you up to now?" he growled. "Why the shackles?"

Willa answered. "You see, it's like this. Pa has a rule. Anyone who sees our diggings either has to be turned into worm food or go to work for us. And since Dorette didn't want you killed, you'll be digging until the cows come home or you keel over, whichever come first."

"Digging what?"

The father walked over to one of several large packs bulging with whatever they contained. Opening the flap, he reached in and pulled out something that he held behind his back as he returned. "Haven't figured it out yet, have you? I prospect for a livin', mister. And this time I've hit the mother lode." He tossed the object in his hand to the ground.

It was one of the largest chunks of solid gold ore Fargo had ever seen. It glittered in the bright sunlight, dazzling to the eye.

"Isn't it a beauty?" the man said. "We have three packs crammed with more just as big." He pointed at the cliff. "And what's best of all is that we haven't even begun to scratch the surface of the vein. By the time we're done, I expect we'll be the richest people in California. Hell, maybe in the whole blamed country."

Willa had lowered the rifle so Fargo saw fit to slowly stand. Dorette, he observed, had made no attempt to help the others. In fact, her expression showed more sympathy than anything else. It was worth keeping in mind. "What happens if I refuse to do as you want?" he asked.

"Then you don't eat or drink, friend," the father said. "If you want to starve yourself to death, that's your business. But take it from me. You won't last long if you don't cooperate."

Fargo wanted nothing more than to get his hands on the

man's throat, or on a gun. "I haven't caught your name yet, friend," he mimicked his captor.

"The handle is Luke Gantry. Not that it would mean anything to you."

"You're the one Veronica Langtree is after."

Gantry reacted as if he had been slapped. "You know that bitch? How? Are you one of her hired guns?"

"I ran into her a few days ago in the Sierra. She claimed that you were a card cheat she was trying to find."

The prospector cackled. "She would. For the better part of a year now she's been hankerin' to get her greedy paws on my claim. Every couple of months she brings her pack of wolves out to the mountains and sniffs around until they run low on coffee and smokes and the like, then they head back to Los Angeles to rest up a spell. I didn't know she was back again." He stared at Ava. "Damn their mangy hides."

Willa poked him with the rifle. "It's all your fault, Pa, sissy being shot. That Langtree woman would never have learned we struck it rich if you hadn't gone off like you did."

"When are you going to quit carpin' about that? One little mistake, and a body never hears the end of it." Gantry gestured in disgust and walked toward the middle of the cliff.

"Little?" Willa lowered her voice, as if confiding in a friend. "He made us give our word never to sneak off. He went on and on about how risky it would be if anyone found out about the vein. And then what did he do? He took off one night when we were all asleep. Went clear to Los Angeles and had himself a grand old time drinking and gambling. He kept his mouth shut, but he spread around too much gold. That Langtree woman became suspicious. Now we have to watch our backs everywhere we go."

Fargo did not feel the least bit sorry for them. They deserved whatever happened. "Tell me," he said. "How many other men have you forced to mine ore?"

"Oh, four or five, not counting Mohaves."

"What happened to them?"

Willa leveled the rifle at a corner of the gorge. "You can see for yourself. Mosey on over to those boulders. And don't try to hoodwink me or I'll put a hole in one of your kneecaps."

Fargo shuffled toward the spot as best he could, burdened as he was by the heavy shackles and chain. He had a fair idea what he would find when he got there, and he was right. Forming a jumbled mound of bleached bones were the skeletons of those who had worn the leg irons before him. He counted eight skulls, seven sporting bullet holes.

"Is your curiosity satisfied, big man?"

"Just fine, thanks." Fargo turned, then stood stock-still. Willa had taken a step to press the rifle muzzle against his groin.

"I almost forgot. You won't have any use for that knife of yours, so hand it over."

Conscious of her finger on the trigger, Fargo bent down. He had to worm his fingers between the shackles and the top of his boot, then pry the toothpick free. She snatched it and stepped back.

"I can see we're going to get along just fine, so long as you keep on behaving yourself."

Fargo was tired of hearing her talk. "How about the food you promised? I won't be any use to you if I'm too weak to lift a shovel."

"Lead the way."

Despite all that had happened, the stew tasted delicious. Fargo downed two heaping helpings, plus four cups of piping-hot black coffee. Willa Gantry was a two-legged viper, but she could cook. She smiled the whole time he ate, and when he was done, she tittered.

"That's some appetite you've got, handsome. I can see I'll have to work extra hard at catching lizards while you're here."

Fargo didn't care what she threw in the pot so long as the concoction filled his belly. He'd eaten lizard before, many times, as well as various kinds of snakes, turtles, and frogs. Even a few insects on occasion, including the time he'd visited a tribe along the Colorado who'd treated him to roasted grasshoppers. At one time or another he had partaken of practically every mammal on the continent, as well, from moose to mice, from bear meat, which the Crows favored, to plump dog, of which the Shoshones were particularly fond. It came of being a frontiersman, of having to make do with what was available at any given time. The wilderness was no place for those with squeamish stomachs.

A low voice intruded on Fargo's reflection, croaking words barely audible.

Ava Gantry had come around. A damp cloth rested on her brow, and Dorette held her right hand. She was staring at the leg irons and saying, "How can you do this to him, Willa? I told you, he saved my life."

"So?" the older sister responded. "We need a new digger. It can't be helped."

Ava was so weak she had to struggle to speak again. "It isn't right. He's not like the rest. Talk to Pa for me. Get him to let Fargo go."

Willa chuckled. "Not on your life, sissy. Pa would tear into me with a switch if I bucked him. No, you talk to him yourself. But you know as well as I do that he won't listen. All he cares about is getting that gold out of the ground."

Ava gazed sadly at Fargo. "I'm sorry, mister. I truly am. I never have liked the idea of making slaves out of every man we meet."

"You've always been too softhearted," Willa chided. "I guess it comes from Pa going easy on you when we were kids because you were the smallest. You've got to learn to be tougher, little sister, if you aim to live to a ripe old age. In this world, only the tough survive."

Dorette, the quiet one, said softly, "Being tough is one thing. Being cruel is another. I agree with Ava."

Willa slapped a hand to her forehead in mock dismay. "Not you, too? What the hell has gotten into both of you? A good-looking cuss comes along and you both fall to pieces on us." She leaned back, sneering. "That's it, isn't it? This has nothing to do with so-called right and wrong. You both fancy him."

"Shut your mouth," Dorette said, barely above a whisper.

"Like hell I will," Willa said. "I want this out in the open."

She laughed, then winked at Fargo. "Tell me, handsome. Do you like your women whole or spoiled?"

"Spoiled?" Fargo repeated, unsure what she was getting at.

Dorette fidgeted. "Don't do this, Willa," she whispered.

"Hush!" the older sister barked. "You're the one making a fool of herself. He'd never be interested in you, and I'll prove it. Take off that bandanna."

The redhead put a hand to her neck. "No."

Willa was enjoying herself immensely. "Haven't you wondered, big man, why my sister there always wears that bandanna around her throat? Why she always talks in a whisper? Even now, when she's mad? There's a reason, you see."

Ava tried to sit up, but couldn't. "Stop it, Willa!" she said. "Don't treat her this way."

"Hush," Willa said. Sliding closer to Dorette, she reached for the bandanna. "If you won't take it off, I'll do it myself."

Meek, shy Dorette turned into a she-cat. Spinning, she slapped Willa's arm aside while simultaneously shoving Willa so hard that Willa tottered back into the fire and scattered burning brands and glowing sparks every which way. Shooting to her feet, Dorette ran off down the gorge, her head hung low, as if in shame.

Fargo figured that Willa would be as mad as a wet hen, but she only chortled. Ava, on the other hand, appeared about to cry. "What was that all about?" he demanded.

Willa stiffled her mirth enough to say, "That fool sister of mine! Dorette can't get it through her thick head that there isn't a man in the world who will take an interest in her, maimed as she is." She burst into louder laughter.

Fargo waited, knowing that Willa was dying to tell him. Knowing, also, that Willa didn't care one bit how much she upset Dorette.

Snorting and slapping her thigh, Willa went on, "About two years ago, when we first began prospecting in this area, we were jumped by a small band of Mohaves. We licked them, but not before one of the bastards put an arrow into Pa's leg and another cut Dorette. Right across the throat. She healed, but all she can do is whisper when she talks. She'll never be the same again."

Ava was watching the retreating figure of their sister. "You're mean, Willa," she said. "Just plain, spiteful mean."

Fargo had a few stronger words he was tempted to use, but he kept his mouth shut. Willa's time would come. Until he could free himself, he had to take pains not to antagonize her or her father, or his skull would wind up in the pile behind the boulders. As if on cue, something thumped against his shoulder, and he twisted to see a shovel lying behind him and Luke Gantry a few yards away.

"On your feet, Fargo. It's time you earned your keep."

The man showed no interest at all in his daughters. He didn't ask how Ava was doing or inquire why Dorette had run off. All that mattered to him was the gold.

Fargo stood, lifting the shovel as he straightened. He had met individuals like Gantry before, both men and women so blinded by the bright yellow ore that greed ruled their every thought, their every act. They would sacrifice anything and anyone at the altar of their golden god, even their own flesh and blood.

Gantry had an old, bulky Walker Colt wedged under his wide leather belt. Drawing it, the prospector waved the pistol at the spot where he had been digging earlier. "Head over there. Be careful not to fall in. I wouldn't want you to break a leg before you fill even one pack."

A gaping pit had been excavated at the base of the cliff. Over twelve feet deep, the only way down was by means of a rickety ladder crudely made from dead tree limbs brought from the mountains. The lower portion of the cliff wall had been exposed, revealing ten or more wide straw-colored veins, enough mineral wealth to fill the treasuries of several countries and still have tons of gold to spare.

"I found it by accident," Gantry commented, as if he were talking to a casual acquaintance instead of someone he held at gunpoint. "We were out on the flats when a dust storm came up, so we ducked into the gorge to wait for the wind to die down. I got bored and was pokin' around back here when I saw a little band of yellow close to the ground. Naturally, I started diggin'." He beamed proudly. "And this is what I uncovered. Old King Midas was a pauper compared to me."

Fargo moved closer to the rim to see the bottom. The ground under him began to give way, with large clods of earth sliding out from under his boots and raining into the pit. He tried to leap to safety but the shackles anchored him, impairing his movement. Another section of dirt broke off. Unbalanced, he teetered, about to fall, when an iron hand fell on his shoulder and he was roughly thrown backward to safety.

"You damn idiot!" Gantry said. "Didn't I tell you to be careful? Do you think I was flappin' my gums for my health? You could bust your fool neck. Then who would do the diggin' for us?"

Fargo was shoved toward the ladder. He gripped the handle of the shovel to swing it, but the Walker Colt rose, pointed at his gut.

"I'd think twice, were I you, friend," Gantry said. "This cannon of mine can put a hole in you the size of a walnut."

Fargo didn't doubt it. The old Dragoons were sometimes unreliable, but those single-action .44's packed a wallop every bit as heavy as current models.

"Climb on down and commence diggin'. You can rest when you're tired, but not for long. If I suspect you're slackin', I'll shoot off a toe or two. You don't need them to shovel with."

There was no getting around it. Fargo cautiously hobbled to the edge, turned, and carefully descended. The ladder shook and shimmied, threatening to break apart if he put too much weight on any one spot. Lying at the bottom was another, shorter shovel, a pick, and a hammer and chisel, everything he would need to mine the ore.

It was grueling work. Fargo had not been at it ten minutes when he was dripping wet. The afternoon sun baked him mercilessly. Soon his throat was parched, his lips so dry it hurt to lick them. He settled into a routine of pounding the pick into the wall to loosen the gold, then prying it out with the chisel and hammer. Gradually a pile grew beside him.

Luke Gantry watched for a while, then left. Fargo did not see him again for a couple of hours, then a cough told him the prospector was back. Gantry noted the size of the pile, grunted approval, then departed once more.

Fargo tired terribly toward the end of the afternoon. The boost of energy the stew had supplied dwindled to nothing, leaving him a fatigued wreck by the time the sun hovered on the western horizon. He had to concentrate just to raise the pick. As he prepared to attack a spur of gold wedged deep in the rock, a tiny stone struck him on the back. He turned.

Dorette was up above, beckoning.

Dropping the pick, Fargo stared at the blisters on his hands before scaling the ladder. His whole body ached. He had to drag himself up the last few rungs, and sank onto his knees to catch his breath. "What is it now?" he asked.

The redhead pointed to the west, where the sun was relinquishing its hold on the heavens. "Time to stop," she whispered. "Supper is about ready."

"And after we eat? Does your father expect me to go back down?"

Again the redhead pointed, this time at a spot over by the burrows where Fargo's bedroll had been spread out. "Not this time," she said as quietly as ever. "I told him you needed lots of rest, after all you've been through. And he agreed."

"Only because he doesn't want me keeling over before I've dug out enough gold to suit him," Fargo guessed. "But we both know that sooner or later I'll wind up like all the rest." Her expression confirmed Fargo's hunch. Uncoiling, he started to rise. Dorette took his elbow to help. He almost shrugged her hand off, he was so mad, but he changed his mind when she gave him a timid smile and whispered in his ear.

"I'm so sorry that you are being treated this way. Really and truly, I am. If it were up to me, we'd let you go this minute."

"Too bad Willa and your father don't see things your way."

"I just wish there was something I could do to help," she said wistfully.

"There is." Fargo nodded at the leg irons. "Sneak me the key."

Panic animated her eyes. "Oh, I don't dare," Dorette breathed. "Pa would beat me within an inch of my life if he caught me."

They were slowly making for the campfire, where Luke Gantry and Willa were huddled by the fire sipping coffee. Fargo bent his head so they couldn't see his lips move. "You talk as if you're different than they are, Dorette. And I take you at your word. But how can you stand by and do nothing when you know damn well what will happen to me, sooner or later? Unless you help me, I'm a dead man."

"You don't know what you're asking. Pa and Willa are *family*. No matter how I feel, I can't betray them. I just can't."

"Would you rather have my death on your conscience the rest of your life?" Fargo was taking a gamble, he knew. Should he push too hard, she might refuse to have anything to do with him. Given the alternative, he had to try to convince her before it was too late.

"I just don't want to talk about it," Dorette declared.

"When can we talk? When I'm lying on the ground with a .44 slug in my skull?"

The redhead stiffened, let go of his elbow, and hustled off toward the horses. Fargo was going to turn and call her back, but her father had taken an interest in them. In order to avoid arousing the man's suspicions, Fargo hobbled to the fire and sank onto his haunches.

Luke Gantry's right hand rested on the butt of the Dragoon. "What were you and Dorette jabberin' about?" he asked gruffly.

"She was telling me how much she likes living in the middle of nowhere with a loco father who doesn't give a damn about his own daughters—" Fargo began, and got no further. The Walker streaked out and up and aligned itself with the tip of his nose.

"It wouldn't be smart to insult me twice, friend," Gantry said. "Most of those dead fellas Willa showed you would still be alive if they had kept that in mind." He pulled back the hammer. "I want the truth. What the hell were you talkin' about?"

Fargo could have lied. He could have made up something believable. But it gave him more pleasure to look Gantry right in the eye and say, "I asked her to help me escape, and she refused. You've got these girls of yours well trained, mister."

Gantry swelled with sadistic glee. "That I do," he boasted, lowering the revolver. "And you'd do well to remember that the next time you try to turn one of 'em against me. All the years I've been searchin' for El Dorado, they've stuck by my side through thick and thin. Their mother, God bless her soul, would be proud of each and every one." He jabbed a thumb toward the horse string. "Look at her now. Doing just as I told her to do."

Fargo swiveled, his brow knitting. Dorette was giving the Ovaro a rubdown. "It's nice of you to be so considerate of my horse," he said dryly.

"Oh, I am," Gantry said. "We'll take real good care of it, for two or three days, at least."

"What happens then?"

The prospector had a toothy grin. "Since you won't be needin' it any longer, we're going to put that pinto of yours to good use." His pause was masterful. "We're going to eat it."

5

Eating horse meat was not all that uncommon on the frontier. Certain Indians did it regularly. The Apaches, for one. They were so partial to horseflesh that they would pamper a horse just to fatten it up for an eventual feast.

But Skye Fargo wasn't an Apache. He had ridden the stallion for so long that he thought of it more as a friend than an animal, in the same way an easterner might regard a devoted dog or cat. Many a time the Ovaro had snatched him from the jaws of death. Together they had gone from Canada to Mexico, from the mighty Mississippi to the Pacific Ocean. And he was not about to sit still and let the pinto be butchered. "Touch a hair on that horse, you son of a bitch, and the first chance I get, I'll split your head with that pick."

Luke Gantry was unimpressed. "Makin' idle threats is a waste of breath, friend." He made a show of hungrily ogling the Ovaro and smacked his lips. "When the time comes, if you ask real nice-like, I might let you have a steak or two."

"Go to hell."

"No, I think I'll go see how much gold you dug for me today." Pleased with himself, Gantry swaggered off, saying over a shoulder, "Feed him, girl. We want him rested and strong in the mornin', so he can work twice as hard."

Supper consisted of the same lizard stew. Willa filled the same bowl he had used before, which had sat in the hot sun all afternoon without being washed. "Eat up, handsome. There's plenty to go around. I bashed in the heads of two big brown lizards about an hour ago. One was downright plump."

Fargo had been famished but his appetite was fading fast.

He spooned a morsel into his mouth and chewed halfheartedly.

Ava was also eating. She smiled and said, "I'm feeling a lot better already. Give me a week and I should be up and around."

"That's nice," Fargo said, not really giving a damn.

"It must have been rough down there," Ava said. "The other men all told me that it gets a little easier as time goes by, if that's any consolation."

Fargo was not about to mince words. "It's not."

Willa clucked several times. "My, my. A few hours of hard work and you just go all to pieces, don't you, big man? I shudder to think what you'll be like tomorrow evening after a full day of digging."

Dipping the spoon a second time, Fargo was about to lift it when a tingle shot through him. Willa had been wearing a thin leather cord round her neck since the day he first saw her. He hadn't given it much thought until now. Since she didn't strike him as the type to go in for fancy jewelry, she had to have something other than a pendant or gem at the end of the cord. It had to be something she wanted close at all times, something she didn't want anyone else to get their hands on.

"What's the matter?" she asked. "You're hardly touching your supper."

Fargo let go of the spoon. "I was thinking of how you threw that hot stew in my face."

Willa laughed in sheer delight. "Lord, you should have seen yourself! I could have split a gut laughing."

"Is that so?" Fargo said casually. "I could use a good laugh right about now." With that, he hurled the contents of his bowl into her eyes and sprang at her as she cried out and automatically swept her hands up to wipe at the clinging mess. Lowering his left shoulder, he rammed into her chest, sprawling her onto her back. Swiftly he gouged a knee into her stomach to hold her down while he tore at her shirt, ripping two or three buttons in his haste.

A large key hung between her bouncing breasts. Fargo grabbed it, pulled, and snapped the leather cord. Stooping, he inserted the key into the shackle on his right ankle. Or tried to. It had to be reversed. As he slid it in, heavy footsteps drummed to his rear.

Luke Gantry's face was a mask of fury. He had drawn the Walker, but instead of aiming it, he held the heavy pistol by the barrel and clubbed it at Fargo's head. Fargo ducked, twisted, and drove his right arm against the prospector's shins. Momentum catapulted Gantry into a tumbling roll. Losing no time, Fargo bent to the leg irons. He gripped the key again.

Screeching like a bloodthirsty cougar, Willa Gantry hurled herself at him, her lips drawn back, her fingers forked. Fargo was bowled onto his back as her hands encircled his throat. With his legs in irons he had to rely on his arms to defend himself. An elbow to the jaw rocked her, and she lost her grip. Clutching her shirt, he flipped her to the left so he could rise.

Her father reared above him. The barrel of the big pistol was gouged into his cheek. Choked with rage, Gantry roared, "Not one twitch or you're coyote bait!"

Fargo wanted his freedom, but not at the cost of his life. He did as the man wanted, offering no resistance as the key was tugged from the leg iron.

Suddenly Willa charged past Luke and kicked at Fargo's head. He jerked back, then covered his face with his forearms as she tried to stomp him into the ground. She was beside herself, livid, uncontrollable. Kicking and stamping, she rained blow after blow, and probably would have gone on doing so until she was too tired to lift her leg had Dorette not appeared and dragged her back against her will.

"I'll kill you for that!" Willa fumed. "You'll be sorry! You're dead! Dead!"

Fargo shut out her curses and rabid raving. He was more concerned about the pistol Luke Gantry still aimed at him. "Shoot me," he said, "and you'll be doing the digging yourself until you can find someone to take my place."

That struck a chord. The prospector's mouth twitched and he shook with suppressed wrath, but he did not squeeze the trigger. "On your feet! For that little stunt, you go hungry tonight. And you'll work twice as hard tomorrow, anyway, or you won't live to see tomorrow night."

Poked and prodded, Fargo was steered to his bedroll and told to lie on his back. From a pack that had been placed nearby, Gantry removed a metal stake, a short length of thin chain, a hammer, and a padlock. The stake was pounded into the ground, the thin chain was looped through the larger chain linking the shackles, and Fargo was padlocked to the stake.

"Just in case you have the notion of runnin' out on us," Gantry baited him.

Fargo was left alone. He rubbed his jaw where Willa had connected with at least one kick. It had been foolish, he told himself, to make his move so soon. He should have waited for a better opportunity to come along. Now they would be doubly cautious, and he had made a vicious enemy of Willa. Sometimes impatience was its own worst enemy.

Willa fumed for an hour, snapping oaths at him from across the camp and vowing to see him dead before the week was out. Fargo had no doubt she would try, whether her father wanted him alive or not.

Stars glittered above. A cool breeze from the northwest had relieved the blistering heat. For the first time all day Fargo wasn't sweating. Be thankful for small blessings, someone had once said. And he was. But it would have been even better had he been free and back in the saddle and on his way north, the Gantrys nothing but a bad memory he would soon forget.

Although he was exhausted, Fargo could not get to sleep. He tried lying on one side, then the other. In time the voices by the fire fell silent. When next he looked, the Gantrys were all stretched out, asleep. The father snored louder than a hibernating bear. Willa was not much quieter.

Fargo knew it was hopeless, but he sat up and tried to free himself anyway. The chains were old and rusted yet still unbreakable. And the stake had been so deeply embedded that he would need to hitch the Ovaro to it to pull it out of the ground. Thwarted again, he lay back down, draped an arm over his eyes, and waited for slumber to claim him. When it did, he felt as if he had been asleep less than five minutes when a warm hand touched his cheek.

Fargo had to struggle to wake up. His sluggish mind tried telling him to forget the hand, that he needed more rest. He came close to drifting off again. Then he detected a scent he knew all too well, the rich, earthy scent of a woman's body close to his, and it had the same effect it always did. His pulse quickened. His senses surged to life. He opened his eyes to find Dorette Gantry lying next to him. Before he could speak, she placed a finger over his lips.

"Keep your voice down," she warned in her customary whisper. "If Pa should catch me, he'll chain me up, too."

To the east the sky bore a faint pink tinge. In under an hour it would be dawn. Fargo twisted to see her better, and his chest brushed her ample bosom. She did not draw away. "What do you want?" he asked.

"I want to strike a deal with you."

Fargo arched an eyebrow. She had insisted that she couldn't bring herself to turn against her own kin. Could it be that she had changed her mind?

"I've been thinking it over," Dorette elaborated. "I'll help you escape, but only if you agree to two conditions."

"Let me hear them."

"The first one will be hard to pull off. I don't want my sisters or my father hurt. You have to give me your word that we'll slip away without harming them."

Fargo almost refused. Luke and Willa deserved to be staked out over ant hills and skinned alive. At the very least, it would give him great satisfaction to pound Luke's head into the ground and give Willa a taste of her own medicine.

His hesitation sparked Dorette to say, "I know how you must feel. But I told you before. They're family. And blood has to count for something. So either you don't lift a finger against them or I don't lift a finger to help you."

"You have my word," Fargo said reluctantly, adding immediately, "What's the second condition?" He wanted her to undo the shackles quickly, before one of the others woke up.

Now it was the redhead's turn to hesitate, as if she were

afraid to mention it. She had the same habit of biting her lower lip that Ava did.

"We don't have all night," Fargo reminded her.

"San Francisco," she blurted.

"What about it?"

"I've always wanted to see it. My second condition is that in return for your freedom, you'll take me there."

It was the last thing Fargo expected. It would delay his reaching Salt Lake City by a week or more. Yet all things being equal, it was a fair request.

"Hear me out," Dorette whispered. "All my life, my pa has been dragging us from one hole in the ground to another, from one godforsaken spot to the next. The Rocky Mountains, the Tetons, the Superstition Mountains, the Mogollon Mountains—we've hunted for gold in all of them."

She paused to check on her father and sisters. Fargo was about to let her know that she did not owe him an explanation when she continued in a rush.

"You must know what it's like to live out in the wild all the time. You must know all the hardships we've had to endure." Dorette grew sorrowful. "There have been times when I've had to go weeks without a bath, times when I've gone a whole year without being able to buy new clothes. I can count on two hands the number of times I've slept under a roof. And I've had to sleep on the hard ground for so long, my elbows and knees have calluses."

"You don't—" Fargo began, but she paid no heed.

"I'm sick to death of living like an animal. I want to live in a bit city, where there are lots of people. I want my own room, with a soft bed and a tub so I can soak until my skin shrivels. I want to be able to go places, to buy nice clothes and all the pretty frills ladies everywhere like, and I want to do it without my pa or my big sister looking over my shoulder all the time." Stopping, she clutched his arm. "Tell me—is that too much to ask?"

"No," Fargo conceded. Her sentiments were much like his own. As much as he enjoyed the wilderness, as much as he felt at home in the high mountains and deep forest, he could no more stand to live like a hermit than he could to become a monk. Civilization had its charms, too. Good sipping whiskey, two-inch-thick beefsteaks, and all-night poker games were just a few he could think of. Not to mention the most important asset of all: sassy, feisty, come-hither women who made a man feel like a prince for a night and gave him fond memories to dwell on around lonely campfires.

"All right," Fargo said. "You have your deal. I'll take you to San Francisco before I head east."

Dorette beamed, then impulsively threw her slender arms around him and kissed him full on the mouth, her silken lips as delicious as the sweetest candy. Her twin mounds massaged his chest, fanning a hunger that had nothing to do with food.

Fargo was almost sorry when she broke off. Remembering he had to keep his priorities straight, he tapped a shackle and urged, "Get these off me before the others wake up."

"I can't."

"What?"

Dorette began to tiptoe off. "I don't have the keys yet. You'll just have to be patient until I can get my hands on them." She blew him a little kiss and was gone.

Just in time. For hardly had Dorette squatted by the embers to rekindle the fire than her father rolled over and sat up, scratching his beard and mumbling to himself.

Fargo had to swallow his disappointment and accept the prospect of another day down in the pit. It wasn't long before Luke Gantry ambled over, the Walker in one hand, the key to the padlock in another.

"Hope you slept well, friend. I expect half a pack of ore out of you today, or I'll know the reason why."

"Only half a pack?" Fargo said sarcastically. "In that case, I might as well sleep in until noon."

"Funny man," Gantry said. "You should be on stage somewhere, makin' folks laugh for a livin'." He tossed the key on the top blanket. "You do the honors. Breakfast is waitin'."

Willa greeted Fargo with a baleful look. She had a large

bruise on her jaw and the top button of her shirt was missing. "Morning, bastard," she growled. "Enjoying one of your last few days on this earth?"

Her father shook a finger at her. "I'll have none of that. I told you last night. Leave him be, Willa Mae, until I say otherwise."

"I owe him, Pa. He hurt me."

"Serves you right. You're the one who talked me into keepin' him, remember? So unless you want to do the diggin' yourself, you'd better behave."

Fargo was handed a familiar bowl filled with familiar contents, only this time the lizard stew was cold. "Don't you ever get tired of the same food over and over?" he complained.

"Sure," Willa said. "That's why we're carving up your horse tomorrow. Or did you forget?"

With all that had gone on since, Fargo was ashamed to admit that he had. He poked at the stew, which was thick enough to use as mortar. Four cups of scalding coffee washed it down. As the sun cleared the horizon, he was led to the hole, and another grueling day of backbreaking labor began.

The bottom of the pit stayed cool longer than the ground up above. For almost an hour Fargo worked in relative comfort. But once the sun rose higher than the rim, the pit became an inferno. Suffocating waves of heat engulfed him. His body broke out in a torrent of sweat. His mouth became unbearably dry. He had to squint against the constant bright glare.

Fargo worked just hard enough to get the job done, and no harder. He lost all track of time. Toward the middle of the morning, as he knelt to pry at a stubborn wedge of gold, a commotion broke out. Hooves pounded. Voices spoke urgently. More hooves drummed. A burro brayed.

Fargo straightened as a shadow fell across the pit. Luke Gantry had a rifle and a bandolier crammed with cartridges. "Company is comin'," he announced. "Mohaves. Willa was off huntin' lizards and spotted 'em enterin' the gorge. Lay low until they're gone. Odds are they won't notice this hole unless they come right up on it."

With that, the prospector dashed from sight.

"Wait!" Fargo called, to no avail. Throwing the pick down, he shuffled to the ladder and climbed. It was slow going with the leg irons, much too slow to suit him, so slow that by the time he climbed high enough to see over the rim, the Gantrys and the horses and the burros were gone. Puffs of dust rising from nearby boulders told him where. Their provisons were right where they had left them, only covered with layers of dirt. From a distance the ruse would work, but not if the Mohaves came close.

Fargo was not about to wait there for the warriors to arrive. If they found him, he'd be easy pickings. The smart thing to do would be to hide among the boulders, where he could defend himself if need be. So, gripping the top rung, he went to pull himself out. He was too late.

Three lithe figures had appeared down the gorge. Gliding like bronze specters over the rough ground, they bounded toward the cliff. Typical Mohaves, they were tall and well-muscled, with thick black hair that hung down to their waists, each wearing a narrow breechcloth. Their bodies were covered with gaudy tattoos. One man had white stripes on his arms and legs, another red hands, the third gray marks on his limbs and chest. Their weapons varied, the first being armed with a bow, the second a club, the third a long lance. They slowed sixty feet out.

The Gantrys had been able to hide themselves and conceal their supplies, but there had not been time for them to erase the many tracks they had made coming and going since they first found the lode. So the Mohaves knew that whites had been there, and recently.

Fargo wondered what Luke Gantry planned to do. Slaying the three warriors invited more trouble, since their tribe would send others to search for them. It amazed him that the family had avoided discovery for so long. Their luck had been bound to run out sooner or later.

The Mohave with the bow had moved out in front of the others. An arrow was notched to the sinew string, ready to fly. Skirting a small boulder, he spied the remains of the hastily extinguished fire. Smoldering embers were giving off telltale wisps of smoke. The archer gestured at his companions, then pointed at the spot. They instantly fanned out, more alert than ever.

On cat's feet the bowman crept to the embers, hunkered down, and lowered a hand to them. They were so hot that he jerked his arm back. The Mohaves now knew beyond any doubt that their quarry had to be very close.

That was the moment Luke Gantry picked to pop up and cut loose, firing three rapid shots at the Mohave nearest him, who happened to be the warrior wielding the war club.

The first slug caught the Mohave in the shoulder, spinning him around. Diving, he flattened behind a boulder as the other rounds whined off into space.

Fargo saw the bowman and the warrior with the lance disappear as if into thin air. Gantry also dropped down again, but the Mohaves knew where he was and would be on him like wolves on a buck. As yet there was no sign of Willa or Dorette. Ava was too weak yet to use a gun and would be left out of the fight.

Silence fell. Nothing moved. Fargo scoured the boulders and clefts for the warriors and finally saw the one with the lance worming along on his belly mere yards from the prospector's hiding place. Gantry's head rose, but he was looking the other way. The warrior drew back his arm, preparing to throw.

Just then, from among boulders a dozen feet beyond the prone Mohave, Willa Gantry reared erect and blasted four shots with her own rifle. At each retort the Mohave reacted as if kicked by a mule. After the last, he rolled onto his back, his eyes wide, and reached in vain for the vault of sky. Stiffening, he died.

It had been a ploy, Fargo realized. Luke had used himself as bait to lure the warriors within range of his daughters. But it wouldn't work a second time. The Mohaves were too clever.

Again silence claimed the gorge. No one showed, not the Gantrys, not the warriors. Fargo thought he heard a horse start to whinny, but the sound was cut short, maybe by a hand clamped onto the animal's muzzle.

Luke reappeared, a score of feet from where he had been. He was facing up the gorge. Suddenly a bow twanged and an arrow missed him by a whisker. He snapped off several shots in the direction the shaft had come from, but it was doubtful he hit the warrior.

Fargo eased a little higher, just enough to see the boulders surrounding Gantry. And just enough, by accident, to see the boulders nearest to the pit. It was hard to say who was more surprised when he saw the wounded Mohave with the club crouched behind one of them. They locked eyes. Fargo hoped the warrior would seek cover elsewhere, but evidently the man figured that Fargo had a gun and was about to use it. Like a tawny panther, the Mohave streaked toward him, whipping the wicked club on high.

Fargo had nowhere to go, no way to escape. He couldn't climb out fast enough to meet the charge, and he couldn't climb down fast enough to evade the club. Somewhere, a rifle boomed. The warrior lurched, but kept his feet long enough to reach the edge of the pit. Fargo brought up an arm to protect himself just as the Mohave came sailing over the rim—and crashed down on top of him.

6

The rickety ladder could barely support the weight of one person. The weight of two shattered it as if it were made from so many twigs, and the next moment Skye Fargo plummeted toward the bottom of the pit with the fierce Mohave on top of him. The warrior had been shot twice, but he was still very much alive. In midair the man swung his big war club and clipped Fargo a numbing blow on the left shoulder as Fargo twisted to get out from under him before they struck the ground.

Then they hit. Fargo had not quite succeeded. His left side bore the brunt. Stunning agony lanced through him, and for a few seconds the pit was a blur. His vision returned quickly. Dazed, he looked up just as the Mohave raised the club for another blow.

Fargo frantically threw himself to the rear. The club thudded within inches of his face. Scrambling backward as rapidly as he could while burdened by the leg irons, he pushed to his knees.

What saved him were the warrior's two wounds. Weakened, losing more blood by the moment, the Mohave was not as fast as he would otherwise have been. The warrior rose slowly, steadied himself, and sprang.

Fargo was still on his knees. In a flash he realized that raising his arms to ward off the club would do more harm than good. The club might break then. And with his arms rendered useless, he would be dead in no time. So, digging his feet into the dirt, hc launched himself down low, at the warrior's legs. His shoulders caught the Mohave above the ankles and brought the man crashing down.

Locked together, they grappled. Fargo got his hands on the club and refused to let go. Tugging and heaving, they each sought to wrest it loose. They rolled first one way, then another. The Mohave's face was red, and blood trickled from his mouth. Fargo wanted to ram his knees into his foe, but the shackles prevented him from raising his legs high enough.

Suddenly the warrior gave a deft flip. Fargo wound up on his back with the Mohave straddling his chest and the club pressing down on his windpipe. The warrior growled, concentrating his efforts on throttling Fargo to death. It took every ounce of strength Fargo had to keep his throat from being crushed.

For perhaps half a minute they waged their silent war. Bit by bit the Mohave was able to force the club deeper into Fargo's flesh. Fargo had to gasp in air to breathe. He bucked. He shoved. He tried to butt the warrior in the face. But he could not dislodge the man.

A grim smile creased the warrior's face. He believed he had won, that in another minute he would rise victorious.

That grin, though, spurred Fargo to greater effort. Fargo was not ready to die, and so long as life remained, he would never give up. Locking his elbows, he shifted to the right, to the left, to the right. The Mohave swayed but did not lose his perch. Shifting to the right yet again, Fargo feinted, pretending to shift left when in reality, at the last instant, he shifted once more even further to the right. It caught the warrior off guard. The man started to slip off Fargo's chest. Seizing the advantage, Fargo drove the end of the club in a tight arc, catching the Mohave across the temple and dumping him in the dust.

Battered and bruised, they rose. Fargo was quicker by a hair. The Mohave had not lost is grip on the club and snapped it at Fargo's stomach, but Fargo sidestepped, balled his hands into a single fist, and brought them smashing down on the bridge of the warrior's nose.

Cartilage crunched, blood spurted, but the Mohave did not go down. The desert did not breed weaklings. The tribe had justly earned its reputation for being one of the toughest in

California. Venting a cry of baffled rage, the warrior planted himself, then swung at Fargo's head.

Air fanned the Trailsman's face as he ducked. His right fist slammed into the Mohave's jaw, his left into the man's cheek. The warrior staggered and retreated a step. Fargo tried to close in, but his left foot became entangled in the chain at his feet. Losing his balance, he lurched, tripped, and sank to one knee.

Splattered with blood, the Mohave swayed upright. He swung the club overhead, but awkwardly, as if he were almost too weak to lift it.

Fargo glanced up. He'd cocked his right arm to punch the warrior in the stomach when the glint of metal drew his gaze to the hilt of a knife wedged under the man's breechcloth. Without thinking, he lunged. His desperate fingers closed on the weapon a heartbeat before the Mohave swept the club at his skull. Throwing himself to the left, he yanked the blade free as the club flashed past his eyes. Then, pivoting, he buried the knife between the warrior's ribs.

The man grunted. That was the only sound he made. Buckling, he oozed to the ground in a disjointed heap, the club thumping to earth beside him.

Fargo took all of five seconds to catch his breath. Pulling the knife out, he wiped it clean on the Mohave's breechcloth, then quickly slid it up his sleeve, blade first.

Up above, all was quiet. Fargo vaguely recalled hearing more shots and yells and the rumble of hooves during his fight. Had the Gantrys won? he wondered. Had they all been killed or driven off? He hesitated to call out in case the only one up there happened to be the Mohave with the bow.

Soft footfalls confirmed that someone was still alive. He moved close to the side where he could see the rim without being seen. The tousled red hair that appeared was a welcome sight.

"Skye?" Dorette leaned out and spotted him. "Thank God! I thought you were a goner. I winged that Indian when he was running toward you, but then I had my hands full for a spell with the other one. He was awful good with that bow of his."

"Get me out of here," Fargo urged. He was worried that her father would force him to stay down there digging until a new ladder could be made. Or that more Mohaves might show up. "There should be a rope on my saddle, unless one of you removed it."

"Hang on. I'll be right back."

But she was gone over three minutes, and every second was an eternity for Fargo. Something told him that he had to get out of that damned pit, and get out right away. Call it gut instinct. Call it a premonition. He paced like a caged panther until she reappeared leading the Ovaro, which she had saddled. One end of his rope had been looped around the saddle horn. The other end she tossed down.

"Here you go. Wrap it around your chest and hold on tight. Holler when you're ready."

Fargo did. Guided by Dorette, the stallion backed from the edge. The rope gouged into him, and the next moment he was hauled smoothly upward. Halfway to the top, he abruptly lurched to a stop. The rope had snagged in a crack.

Dorette bent to take stock of the situation. "I think I can free it," she whispered loudly. Stooping, she kicked at the cleft, dislodging clods of earth, widening the gap so the rope could slide freely.

All Fargo could do was hang there, helpless, and pray she finished before Luke noticed what she was up to. Some of the dirt raining down pelted him on the head and shoulders, but he didn't complain. The important thing was to get out of that pit right away.

Dorette rose, gripped the Ovaro's bridle, and smacked the pinto on the shoulders. Muscles rippling, the big stallion moved forward step by deliberate step, raising Fargo higher, ever higher, until he could grab the lip and hike himself over the rim. For a few moments Fargo's legs dangled, and if not for the rope he would have lost his hold and fallen. At a whispered command from Dorette, the Ovaro took several more strides. Fargo was pulled a couple of feet on his belly. When he stopped, solid ground supported him.

"We did it!" Dorette said happily, rushing back to help him stand. "Are you all right?"

Fargo, nodding, scanned the gorge. It was empty, save for the dead Mohave Willa had shot. "Where's your father? And your sisters?"

"Ava is over behind those boulders with the animals," the redhead said. "Pa and Willa rode after that Injun with the bow. He put up a good scrap, but he didn't stand a chance against all our rifles. So he ran off."

Fargo knew better. The warrior was no fool. Outnumbered he had done what any prudent man would have done—he had gone for help. Unless Luke and Willa caught him, the warrior would return in a few days with a large war party. "Were you able to get the key to the leg irons?" he asked.

"Not yet. Willa watches it like a hawk. I think maybe she suspects I'm up to something."

"Find me a hammer and chisel."

Dorette gnawed her lower lip. "Are you sure that's wise? They're bound to come back before you're done. Pa will fly into a rage and we'll both be punished. I'm supposed to be guarding you, after all."

Fargo's last shred of patience was gone. He was not going to spend another minute as their slave, no matter what. A twist of the wrist was all it took to drop the knife down his sleeve into his hand. Reversing his grip, he lightly pressed the keen tip to her side. He would never stab her, but she didn't know that.

"What are you—?" she blurted.

"I'll take this," he announced, snatching her rifle, a Spencer, from the crook of her elbow. "Now find me a hammer and chisel. And hurry. If your father catches us, our deal is off."

Dorette was so mad, she sputtered. "You're making a mistake. You could ruin everything."

"Time is wasting," Fargo stressed. Spinning her around, he swatted her fanny. "Move!" She frowned but hurried toward the boulders. He followed at a hopping run, the chain rattling noisily, and checked to verify the Spencer had a round under the hammer. Skirting the foremost boulders, he halted beside a flat one the size of a washbasin.

The rest of the horses and the burros were tied in a row. Ava sat with her back to a saddle, a rifle across her lap. She was awake and smiled at him. "I'm glad that savage didn't get you. Dorette and I were awful worried."

The redhead had her nose in a pack. "Where is it?" she was saying. "I know we had a spare in here." Her arm flapped around inside.

Fargo rose on the tips of his toes to gaze up the gorge. So far her father and the older sister were nowhere in sight. How soon they returned depended on how successful the Mohave was at eluding them.

"Here it is!" Dorette exclaimed softly, holding aloft a chisel. A hammer in her other hand, she scooted to the flat boulder. "Couldn't you just shoot the shackles off?" she asked.

"And have a bullet ricochet into my leg? No thanks," Fargo answered. Taking the tools, he placed the edge of the chisel against the lock on the right shackle, aligned the hammer, and swung. He was prepared for the pain, or so he thought. The circle of rusty iron wrenched sharply, its upper and lower edges biting into his leg. Gritting his teeth, he applied the hammer again and again, the sound of the blows echoing off the high gorge walls.

"That will take forever," Dorette commented.

She was right. Fargo swung harder. The chisel bit into the iron but not deeply. Changing tactics, he inserted it into the thin crack between the two halves of the shackle. A resounding blow racked his foot and leg with agony, but it also widened the crack a fraction. Encouraged, he redoubled his effort. By gradual degrees the two halves separated.

Dorette was keeping watch. Ava, to his surprise, had stood, and using her rifle as a crutch, hobbled over to watch him.

It soon became apparent to Fargo that the leg irons were too sturdily built to shatter. Yet all was not lost. He continued to spread the two sections apart. Presently he widened them to where he might be able to slip his foot through the opening.

Sitting, he removed his boot and tried. It took a lot of wriggling and cost him patches of skin, but soon his foot popped free.

"You did it!" Ava squealed.

Fargo applied himself to the other leg iron. It proved more stubborn, but at length he slipped his foot from the clamp, stood, and cast the shackles as far from him as he could. Sitting to put his boots back on, he glanced at the redhead. "Fetch my guns."

His tone let her know he would brook no argument. From her bedroll she removed the Henry and the Colt and brought them over. "Where's my toothpick?" he asked, while twirling the pistol into his holster.

"Willa has it, I think."

Fargo worked the Henry's lever, satisfied himself it was loaded, and set it down next to him. "Saddle your horse and fill your saddlebags with whatever you want to take. We're leaving in about two minutes. Ava should be safe here until your father and sister get back."

Dorette looked at her younger sibling, who gestured "Umm, about Ava. She feels pretty much the same way I do. I knew that I could trust her, so I confided that you're taking me to San Francisco. Now she wants to come along, too."

About to tug on his left boot, Fargo paused. He liked Ava, but she was still too weak from her wound to be able to hold her own on a long trek. Her presence would be more of a hindrance than a help. She would slow them down, for one thing. Still, he couldn't bring himself to come right out and say no. "Are you sure that's wise?" he brought up.

"Maybe not," Dorette said. "But this is the first chance either of us has ever had to start over again, and we aim to take it. If you don't want her to tag along, ride on out by yourself. I won't hold you to your promise. Ava and I will manage on our own."

"I didn't say I wouldn't keep my word," Fargo said testily. Slipping his second boot on, he stood and stomped his feet a few times. Ava was staring at him, but he wouldn't meet her gaze. He was wise to female wiles.

"I can go, then?" Ava spoke.

"I didn't say that, either," Fargo hedged.

"What are you saying, exactly? Either I can or I can't. Make up your mind. My pa won't be gone much longer."

Fargo disliked being boxed in a corner. They knew damn well he couldn't refuse if they insisted. "Are you fit enough to spend the next seven to ten days in the saddle?"

"I won't know until I try," Ava responded. "All I can promise is that I'll do my best not to be a burden." She rested her warm fingers on his. "Please, Skye. You must know how much this means to me. I'll get down on my knees and beg, if that's what it takes."

Shrugging her hand off, Fargo claimed his Henry. "I know I'm going to regret this." They giggled like two girls about to go on their first date as he headed for the Ovaro. "Pack up and meet me at the first bend. With any luck, we can cross Death Valley by nightfall."

It felt wonderful to fork leather again. Fargo held onto the Henry. Promise or no promise, he was not going to let Luke Gantry clamp those leg irons on him a second time. He'd rather die first. At a trot he rode to a point where he could see clear to the mouth of the gorge. Other than a lizard that streaked into the shadows, nothing moved.

The women took longer than Fargo had planned on. Fully five minutes went by. He was about to hasten back and find out what was keeping them when they galloped out from behind the boulders, the redhead leading a burro burdened with packs and blankets. As they clattered up, he jabbed a thumb at the extra animal. "What the hell is that?"

"Supplies and stuff," Dorette said.

"That donkey can't possibly keep up with the horses," Fargo informed her. "Leave it here. We'll make do."

"The provisions will come in handy. Let's at least try." This from Ava.

Fargo was growing tired of having to debate every decision. The burro fidgeted, twisting its head to nip at one of the straps holding the packs in place. Its legs were spaced wide apart in just the sort of stance he had seen donkeys adopt when carrying too much weight. Suspecting the truth, Fargo nudged the Ovaro next to the smaller animal, leaned down, and opened the flap on one of the packs. Gold ore glittered in the sunlight. He counted three similar packs.

"Are the two of you sunstruck? Your father and Willa will catch us in no time if we try to lug this along. We have to travel light."

"What can a little hurt?" Ava rejoined.

"A handful of nuggets would be a little," Fargo said. "You've brought enough to make yourselves the richest women in San Francisco."

"That's the general idea," Dorette whispered.

In a flash of insight, Fargo understood. "You planned this all along. You intended to leave with as much gold as you could bring."

"What if we did?" Dorette said. "Can you blame us? How can we make a new life for ourselves if we don't have any money? With these packs we can set ourselves up in grand style, just like those rich ladies we've heard tell of. We can buy all the things we could never afford before. Clothes, carriages, a big mansion. You name it."

Fargo lifted the reins. "It wasn't part of our bargain. If you're coming, fine. But leave the burro behind." To nip another argument in the bud, he pricked the pinto's flanks with his spurs and trotted on down the gorge. It bothered him to learn that Dorette and Ava were every bit as greedy as Luke and Willa, but he shouldn't have been surprised. They hadn't stayed with their father all those years out of a sense of daughterly duty.

Fargo did not look back until he was almost to the opening. The sisters were following. Not happily, but they were coming. He drew rein and rose in the stirrups to survey the arid flatland that stretched miles eastward to the foothills of the Panamint Mountains. Six miles, he estimated. They could reach the range before dark.

Fargo thought to check if Dorette had brought a water skin. She had, so without further delay he cantered into the open. The sizzling heat was as stifling as ever. He had not gone more than a quarter of a mile when he removed his bandanna to mop his brow. The women were strung out in single file behind the pinto, Ava in the middle. Dorette had shoved the Spencer into her boot.

It seemed to Fargo that for once luck was with him. Since the Mohave heartland lay to the south, he figured that the surviving warrior had led Luke and Willa on a merry chase in that direction along the base of the Amargosa, the range bordering Death Valley to the east. He would reach the mountains to the west, the Panamints, long before they even returned to the gorge.

About halfway across, Fargo slowed. Pushing the horses too hard in that heat might cause one of the animals to go lame, and they could ill afford to lose a single mount.

They had covered close to four of the six miles, and the snow on the crags of the Panamints beckoned like the inviting beacon of a lighthouse, when spiraling tendrils of dust appeared on one of the lower slopes. Growing rapidly, the tendrils blossomed into a cloud that wound down to the bottom of the mountains and without delay struck out across Death Valley. Directly toward Fargo and the two women. He promptly halted.

Ava was also aware of the cloud. "Who are they?" she wondered. "More savages?"

"Mohaves always travel on foot," Fargo reminded her. There could be no doubt the newcomers were on horseback, and that there were a lot of them.

"Maybe they're friendly," Dorette whispered, but even she did not sound convinced.

Fargo had to make up his mind quickly. Going back was out of the question. They ran the risk of encountering Luke Gantry and Willa. Heading north also posed a problem. Judging by the angle at which the riders were approaching, they would be cut off before they could break into the clear. Riding eastward would have the same result. That left one direction to take, the very last direction anyone in his right mind would take. Due south. Deeper into Death Valley. And toward Mohave territory.

"What do we do?" Ava asked anxiously.

In response, Fargo wheeled the Ovaro and fled south. He saw no cause for worry. Their horses were well rested. They had a wide lead. Plus all three of them had rifles and ample ammunition. His plan was to outdistance their pursuers, then swing westward into the Panamints. Once they reached the high country, there would be plenty of water and game.

Dorette rode superbly. Ava, though, had lost what little color she had regained in her cheeks and was holding onto her saddle with both hands. Fargo watched her closely, convinced she would not last long.

Half an hour passed. The horses were lathered with sweat and beginning to tire. The dust cloud didn't gain on them, but neither had they been able to pull ahead, as Fargo would have liked. Ava grew steadily weaker.

Fargo stayed close to her sorrel in case she lost her grip. Focused as he was on her, he didn't pay as much attention as he should have to what lay ahead of them until Ava pointed and called out.

"What's that?"

It was another dust cloud. And like the first, it was coming straight toward them.

7

Skye Fargo slowed the Ovaro, but his mind raced. The second dust cloud was a lot smaller than the first and was approaching from the southeast. It was far enough off that if they bore to the southwest and pushed their animals as hard as they dared, they might be able to evade those making the cloud.

"It must be Pa and Willa," Ava guessed.

Fargo had the same idea. And he had no doubt the pair would open fire on him the second they came within range. "This way!" he said, pointing to the southwest and applying his spurs.

On they raced, the sun broiling them mercilessly, their animals all too rapidly reaching the brink of exhaustion. Of the three horses, the Ovaro had the best endurance, but even the superb stallion had its limits.

Ahead, Death Valley narrowed, thanks to a spur of the Panamint Mountains. Fargo reasoned that if they could reach that spur far enough ahead of their pursuers, they stood a good chance of losing themselves in the trees. At the very least, the vegetation would afford cover. They could defend themselves a lot better than they could out in the open. But could they get there in time? The dust cloud to their rear was much closer, and Luke and Willa Gantry had veered to cut them off. It would be close.

To complicate matters, Ava's strength was ebbing fast. She was barely able to hang on. Once again she had stuck her boots through the stirrups. She had also lashed the reins around her wrist. As if that were not enough, bending low, she had entwined her other hand in the sorrel's mane.

For long minutes the chase went on. The Panamints grew

close enough for Fargo to make out individual trees. A confident smile creased his lips, to die prematurely when a small knot of riders burst out of the vegetation at the point where the mountain and Death Valley met. There were only three, but they held rifles that gleamed like shiny spears in the sunlight. The tall man in the lead wore a wide-brimmed black hat.

Fargo immediately bore to the south and the women followed suit. Now he knew who was after them. That rider with the black hat had to be Dee Trench, which meant that the main group of gunmen was behind him, led by the beautiful Veronica Langtree herself.

It was not hard for Fargo to figure out what had happened. Since it undoubtedly had been one of Langtree's hired killers who'd bushwhacked Ava, Langtree and company had followed her trail and eventually stumbled on the spot where Fargo and Ava had camped. From there, Langtree had followed the tracks eastward, but lost them at some point. By then Veronica would have realized that she had been mistaken, that Gantry's strike wasn't in the Sierra but somewhere in or near Death Valley. She had camped in the foothills, biding her time, and spotted Fargo and the women as they crossed. Ordering Trench and two others to parallel the valley in the event Fargo got past her, she had given chase.

The woman didn't miss a trick.

And now Fargo was in a worse fix than ever. To his left were the crazed prospector and the bloodthirsty bitch who wanted nothing more than to slit his throat. To his right were three hardened gunmen who would fill him with lead without a second thought. Behind him was a coldhearted temptress who would do anything to get her hands on the prospector's gold. And as if all that were not enough, second by second he was heading deeper into the heart of Mohave territory.

Some days it just didn't pay to roll out of the sack.

The crack of a rifle shattered Fargo's reverie. Dee Trench had fired. The slug raised a dust swirl dozens of yards short of Fargo and the sisters. Motioning, Fargo let the women get in front of him. Then, twisting in the saddle, he tucked the Henry to his shoulder and rose in the stirrups to reduce the swaying effect of the pinto's rolling gait. Steadying his arms, he sighted, thumbed back the hammer, and squeezed the trigger.

The range was a little too great. Fargo missed, but not by much. Dust kicked up almost in front of Trench's mount, causing the tall gunman and his companions to slant to the west. They slowed, unwilling to challenge Fargo's marksmanship a second time.

Luke and Willa Gantry had also slowed. They were visible at last, Willa with her telescope out. Fargo figured that she had spotted him and the other two and ridden to intercept them, totally unaware of Langtree's outfit. Now that they knew, what would they do? Come to the aid of Dorette and Ava? Or think only of the gold?

There was never any doubt. Luke and Willa reined around and sped toward the Amargosa Range, toward the gorge and their precious pit.

Moments later, the large dust cloud being made by Langtree and her riders split in half. The cloud that separated veered after the fleeing pair. Shots were exchanged, but Luke and Willa did not appear to be hit.

Trench and the others had fallen back, perhaps so the main group could catch up to them.

Meanwhile, Fargo galloped to the south. He did not know how much farther Death Valley extended, but he did know that sooner or later they would come to its mouth and beyond would lie endless miles of the burning desert men called the Mojave. A vast wasteland larger than most states back East, it was one of the most inhospitable places on the face of the planet.

It soon became apparent that their pursuers were no longer in any great rush to overtake them. Trench rejoined those still after them.

Try as Fargo might, he could not tell if Langtree was among them, or whether she had gone after Luke Gantry. He slowed to a trot, content to maintain his lead for the time being since it was the best he could do under the circumstances. Another mile fell behind them, then two. Death Valley widened again.

They could not reach either mountain range without being caught.

It was late in the afternoon when they came on a dry wash over ten feet wide and six feet deep. A gradual slope brought them to the bottom. There, Fargo drew rein and slid from the saddle. "Climb down and rest," he directed. "We're staying here until dark."

"But what about those men after us?" Dorette asked. "They'll catch us if we don't go on."

"Not if I can help it."

Climbing back to the top, his boots slipping and sliding in the loose gravel, Fargo knelt and pulled his hat brim low against the blinding sun. Trench and five hard cases were several hundred yards out, coming on warily. From the manner in which they were looking every which way, they were puzzled. Fargo rested the barrel of his rifle on the rim. The nearest gunman was a scruffy character armed with a Sharps, and Fargo took a bead on the center of the man's barrel chest. Sweat dribbling down his face, he waited, letting them get closer, so close that he could see the whites of the man's eyes when he stroked the trigger.

At the blast of the Henry, the gunman was flung from his mount and smashed onto his back to lie as still as a log. The rest promptly darted to the right and the left, firing wildly on the fly.

Fargo tracked a second rider, led him just a hair, and fired. The man jerked at the tearing impact of the slug but somehow stayed on his horse and rode on out of range.

Trench and one or two others pinpointed Fargo. A ragged volley split the hot air. Bullets smacked into the dirt all around him. Lead hornets buzzed overhead. He was forced to duck. When the firing slackened, he raised up, but by then most of them were too far out. They gathered in a knot and dismounted to tend to the wounded man.

"That should make them think twice before they try anything."

Fargo had not heard Dorette join him. She held the Spencer at her side, her thumb on the hammer. Her wind-tossed red hair and the smooth sheen of moisture on her face lent her a natural, untamed quality that Fargo liked. Her soaked blouse clung to her figure, highlighting the outline of her breasts and her flat stomach. Her willowy thighs were also stained with perspiration and he couldn't help but imagine what they would look like unclothed.

Ava was with the horses, seated with her back to a boulder. She smiled weakly at him, then closed her eyes.

"How is she holding up?" Fargo asked.

"Better than you think. Don't worry. She's a lot tougher than she looks."

Peeking over the lip, Fargo confirmed that Trench and the others were content to stay where they were for the time being. "I could go for some water," he mentioned.

Dorette went for the water skin. She allowed her sister to drink before climbing the slope. Fargo shook his head when she offered it to him.

"Ladies first."

"Thank you, kind sir," Dorette quipped. She knew enough not to guzzle but drank sparingly, sipping to wet her lips and then swallowing small amounts to slake her thirst.

The sun hung an hour above the horizon. Fargo studied the lay of the land while taking his turn at the water skin. From where he sat, he could not say if the dry wash, which ran from east to west, went all the way to the Panamint Mountains. If so, it was the first lucky break they'd had. He explained what he had in mind while Dorette kept her eyes on the gunmen.

Ava had fallen asleep. The reins to their three horses had slipped from her fingers, but the animals were too tired to run off. All three stood with their heads low to the ground, their tails flicking feebly.

Fargo capped the water skin and set it beside him. Beads of moisture had formed on the outer surface. By wiping a palm from top to bottom he collected enough to dab cool drops on his neck and cheeks. It felt wonderful.

The redhead crouched next to him. "I'd like to cool off, too," she whispered.

Thinking that she would rather do it herself, Fargo started to lift the bag to place it at her feet.

"No. You do it for me."

The playful grin she wore convinced Fargo she was serious. Smiling, he rubbed both hands the length of the water skin, getting them good and wet, then touched his palms to her face. Her skin, like his, felt as if it were on fire. Slowly, teasingly, he ran his hands down over her chin to her neck. When she made no protest, he worked them lower, sliding them over her collarbones, to the tops of her full breasts. Her grin widened. It reminded him of his long-standing belief that women had a knack for picking the damnedest times to get romantic. For all their talk about doing what was prim and proper, most women were secretly minxes at heart once they let their hair down, so to speak. He would have liked to dip lower, but he didn't want to start something he couldn't finish then and there.

"That was nice," Dorette whispered as he dropped his arms. "I bet you can massage a girl's troubles clean away."

"I can try," Fargo proposed. He was curious as to what had sparked her passion, but he knew better than to quiz her. Women liked to play at being mysterious. It added to the allure, to the thrill they got out of making love to a man. "Once we get out of this mess."

Dorette's brow furrowed. "I hope Pa and Willa are all right. If that Langtree bitch gets her hands on them, she'll make them suffer before she finishes them off."

Fargo would not come right out and say it, but he felt no sympathy at all for Luke or Willa. Had the redhead not made him give his word that he'd spare them, he would have waited back at the gorge and put a slug into each of them when they returned. And even that would have been too good for them. They did not deserve a quick, painless death. Justice demanded that they have their necks stretched. Unfortunately, the nearest law was hundreds of miles away, in Los Angeles.

"Listen," Dorette said.

The thud of hooves drew Fargo to the rim. Two of the gunmen were leaving, one heading west, the other to the east. The reason was plain. Trench had sent them to swing wide to either side, where they would lay low in the event Fargo and the sisters tried to reach either mountain range under cover of darkness.

Dorette also figured it out. "They're cutting off our escape."

"Nor quite," Fargo said, gazing to the south, the one avenue still open to them. Was it by chance, or were the cutthroats herding them toward Mohave country on purpose? In the distance the high peaks dwindled, showing they were much too close for comfort to the end of Death Valley.

As if the redhead were reading his thoughts, she remarked, "We can't go that way. Hardly anyone ever goes into the Mojave Desert and comes out again."

Ava picked that moment to stir and sit up. Dorette carried the water bag to her, leaving Fargo alone with his thoughts. He reloaded the Henry, then checked on Trench. The three killers had ground-hitched their mounts and were seated in the meager shade their animals provided.

The sun sank much too slowly. Fargo lost track of the two gunmen that had been sent to outflank them. It was as if the earth had swallowed the pair up. Or else they had dropped down into the dry wash, which in itself posed a new threat since now they could work their way toward him without being seen.

As the blazing orb dipped from the sky, a stiff wind picked up from the northwest, whirling dust devils high into the air and stinging Fargo's face with bits of sand and dirt every time he rose high enough to see the plain. Twilight was brief. The darkness deepened to where he could barely make out the women below him.

Sliding to the bottom, Fargo crouched beside them. Ava was sitting up, but she had an arm pressed to her side and her features were haggard. "Are you up to a hard ride?" he asked.

"Try me."

Fargo examined the horses, running his hands up and down the legs of each. One of the sorrel's was slightly swollen above the fetlock. They risked losing the animal if they weren't careful.

The women came over as Fargo removed his rope from his saddle. Throwing a loop over the sorrel, he handed the coils to Dorette. "This way the two of you won't be separated," he instructed her.

"What about you?"

Before Fargo could reply, the stallion raised its head, its ears pricked, and stared fixedly along the wash to the east. Fargo had heard nothing, but he had learned long ago to rely on the pinto's enhanced senses. Giving the redhead a push, he said urgently, "Help your sister up!"

Down the wash, a pebble clattered. Fargo spun as fireflies flared. A rifle spoke three times. He answered with two shots of his own, aiming at the gun flashes. There was a yelp and the firing stopped, but only for a few seconds. To the west, the other flanker joined the fray, his rifle louder. Slugs cleaved the air and the skittish sorrel pranced in fright. Fargo worked the lever of his Henry three times. The third retort was greeted by a strangled cry. Then the night quieted.

In a long stride Fargo reached the Ovaro. Gripping the saddle horn, he swung aloft. The south rim was a black silhouette against the backdrop of sky and stars. "Now!" he said, bending to slap the sorrel's flank. Ava clung on for dear life as her horse scrambled up the bank, dirt spewing in its wake. Dorette had to follow so as not to lose her hold on the rope. Fargo went up last. As the pinto gained level ground, more shots peppered the night, coming from the north. He heard Trench and the last two gunmen bearing down on the wash. Swiveling, he trained the Henry on a cluster of dusky figures and banged off a pair of swift shots. A horse whinnied. A man cursed lustily. Fargo whirled and headed out after the women, who had a twenty-yard lead.

Additional shots rocked Death Valley, some from the east, some from the west. The killers in the wash were very much alive.

Fargo did not bother wasting ammo. He rode like the wind, his shoulder blades prickling, half expecting to feel the searing anguish of hot lead ripping through him at any second. In a short while the gunfire faded. He shoved the Henry into the saddle scabbard, then flicked the reins to overtake the women. They maintained a brisk clip, Ava swaying every now and then. Worse, her sorrel showed definite signs of going lame.

Fargo moved up close to the redhead. "We'll push on as long as we can," he said, knowing that he doomed the sorrel by doing so. But it was crucial they widen their lead while they could. Trench would not give up easily.

Across the starlit landscape they galloped. Soon Fargo saw that mountains no longer framed them on either side. They had left Death Valley behind. Ahead stretched trackless miles of empty desert. The time had come to swing westward and loop back into the Panamint range. He gripped the reins, about to turn. As a simple precaution he glanced back.

Shadowy shapes flitted in spectral pursuit.

Fargo bent low and kept on going. Pacing the women, he marked how the sorrel favored its front leg. It would not be long before the limb gave out, forcing Ava to ride double with her sister. Their combined weight would soon prove too much for Dorette's winded animal, leaving them no better off. Trench would catch them in no time.

There had to be an alternative.

Ahead and to the right rose what appeared to be a series of low hills. Only then did Fargo recall hearing that many small isolated mountain ranges and extinct volcanoes dotted the Mojave Desert. It gave him hope. Taking the lead, he made for the barren heights. Low ridges rose around him, giving way to stark peaks. Ridges and arroyos crisscrossed their path. The result was a maze of rocky crests and stone crags.

At length Fargo stopped. The rattle of their hooves died, to be replaced by the chill sigh of the brisk breeze. He listened until assured that Trench had lost track of them.

A ravine that Fargo thought might offer a hiding place instead lead to a jagged bluff they skirted. On the far side, amid a forest of jumbled boulders, in a draw with steep walls, Fargo called a halt. There was no spring, but they still had the water skin.

Dorette helped him make Ava comfortable. She also lent a hand stripping the saddles and blankets from their mounts.

Fargo checked the sorrel and was not surprised to learn that its leg was twice as swollen as before. He allowed each horse three handfuls of water.

Ava had fallen asleep by the time Fargo was done. While Dorette covered her, he helped himself to a few pieces of pemmican and walked down the draw. A mound of boulders served as stepping stones to a low shelf with an unobstructed view of the draw opening. He had noticed it on the way in.

Fargo propped the Henry against the wall, wearily sank down, and took a bite. He was famished. But he was so tired that he didn't feel much like eating.

The scuff of a shoe whipped Fargo into a crouch. A lithe form glided up the boulders toward him, and had he not seen long hair waving in the wind, he would have fired. "Are you trying to get yourself shot?" he grumbled as the redhead boosted herself up beside him.

"I thought you might like some company."

Fargo put the rifle down. "Shouldn't you be keeping an eye on your sister?"

"She's fine. There's no fever, no sign of bleeding. By morning she'll be raring to go." Dorette moved to the edge of the shelf. "You picked a good spot. They'll never find us in here."

"Never take anything for granted," Fargo cautioned. Leaning back, he made himself comfortable. "I'll keep first watch and wake you about midnight. You'd be smart to get some rest while you can."

"I'm not tired," Dorette whispered, sinking down so close next to him that their legs brushed. As if by accident, her hand fell onto his thigh. She made no attempt to move it.

Skye Fargo almost laughed aloud. Who did she think she was fooling? Women liked to pride themselves on being as devious as foxes. But the truth was that they were as obvious as randy elk once they made up their minds they wanted a man. He stared at her bosom, gauging by the twitch in his loins whether to let her have her way or send her packing.

She was in luck.

"I've been thinking," Dorette said.

"About what?" Fargo asked. As if he couldn't guess.

"All you've done for us. Most men would have skedaddled as soon as they were free of those shackles, but not you. You stuck by your word."

"Don't make me out to be more than I am."

Dorette leaned forward, bringing those rosy lips of hers within inches of his. She stared at him as if expecting him to act. When he didn't, she frowned.

"Is something wrong?" Fargo asked innocently. He was enjoying himself immensely. Her antics qualified as the most amusing thing to happen to him in days.

"I thought you liked me."

"I do."

"Really liked me," Dorette stressed, bending further, her warm breath on his mouth, her earthy scent intoxicating. "You even promised to give me a massage."

"I did?" Fargo played dumb. She pursed her lips in annoyance and started to back away. Laughing, he grabbed her wrist, yanked her across his lap, and pressed his chest to hers.

"You bastard. You were playing with me."

"Guilty as charged," Fargo admitted. "But now it's time to get serious." So saying, he swooped his hands to her breasts and covered her mouth with his.

8

Skye Fargo felt Dorette Gantry tense in fleeting surprise at the sudden flare of his passion. But as his tongue parted her soft lips to slip into her silken mouth, she relaxed under him, her arms curling around his neck, her fingers entwining in his hair. Their tongues met and danced together, hers tasting as sweet as the headiest of nectars.

Fargo's hands were also busy. He squeezed her breasts, feeling them swell, feeling the taut nipples harden even through her shirt. She had big nipples. Sensitive nipples. When he tweaked one, she squirmed. When he tweaked both, she cooed and ground her hips against him, enticing him to do more. He was all too willing to oblige. Kneading her mounds, he soon had her quaking with unbridled desire from head to toe.

Fargo broke the kiss to trace his lips over her cheek to an earlobe. He sucked and flicked, then lathered her neck to the fluttering base of her throat. Shifting, he laid her flat and stretched out beside her. She nipped at his chin. Her mouth found his ear; her hot breath fanned it.

Fargo's right hand roved lower, across her tummy to the junction of her thighs. She parted her legs for him, but he did not let his fingers go any lower. Not yet. He wanted to savor the moment, to heighten her excitement by drawing out the suspense. Rubbing her nether mound, he eased a knee between her thighs. She clamped them around his leg to hold him in place, as if she were afraid he might yet change his mind.

There was nothing to fear on that score. Fargo needed the release, needed to forget about the hardships of the past few days. Her lush body promised pleasure beyond compare, and he meant to indulge himself fully. Like a starved man at a banquet, he was going to feast on her nubile bounty until he had gorged himself.

Gone was the awful heat of the day. A welcome cool breeze wafted over them, adding to their pleasure. Fargo removed his hat and placed it beside the Henry, then worked off the redhead's boots. Tugging her shirt out from her pants, he slipped a hand underneath, onto her tight stomach. It quivered at his touch.

Their mouths met again, and locked. She swirled her tongue around his. He caught hers between his lips and sucked as he might on hard molasses. The taste was indescribably delicious. His right hand, caressing her ribs, came to the sloped globe of her exquisite breast. Lightly, he massaged it. Her skin grew warm, then hot. Her nipple resembled a small nail, peaked with raw lust. He pinched it, causing her bottom to come up off the rock shelf and lift his along with it. A throaty purr rumbled from deep in her chest.

The purr changed to a moan when Fargo slid his other hand up her shirt to join the first. Covering both globes, he squeezed. She wriggled and sighed contentedly. For the longest while he dallied there while his mouth and hers stayed glued to one another. The whole time, his carnal hunger mounted. His manhood became a pole, straining for release. His senses swam, as if he were giddy from too much liquor. But it was intoxication of another sort, of a better sort, of the kind that men and women had longed to experience since the dawn of the race.

Fargo undid her shirt, exposing her lustrous skin. It broke out in goose bumps as he rubbed his hands over every square inch. She had a sheen about her, a glow almost. Perhaps it came from having always lived outdoors. Or perhaps it was simply part of her sensual allure. Whatever, she literally throbbed with sexual vitality.

Easing lower, Fargo kissed and nibbled a path from her jaw to her right breast. He encircled the nipple, then flicked it with vigor. Her nails dug into his shoulders. Eyes hooded, she smacked her lips. Fargo gave the other mound the same treatment. His right hand went around her back to trace the outline of her spine from her shoulders to her buttocks. Cupping the latter, he mashed his loins against hers, letting her feel how hard he was, how ready.

Somewhere off in the Mojave a coyote yipped. Elsewhere, a night bird screeched. Those were the only sounds other than the wind and the heavy panting of the redhead.

Fargo unfastened her pants and hitched them down her long legs. As he tossed them aside, the sight of her full, glass-smooth thighs took his breath away. It was as if they had been sculpted from the finest marble by a master sculptor. He stroked them, stopping shy of her core. After a while he just had to kiss them, so he knelt between her legs and did so. Her skin was as creamy as milk, as sheer as satin. He could not get enough of those thighs.

A new, dank scent increased Fargo's yearning. Like a hummingbird drawn to honey water, he nuzzled into her crack and tasted the sweet dew seeping from her nether lips. His mouth molded to her tunnel. His tongue alighted on the tiny knob at its rim.

Dorette gasped. She grasped him by the shoulders and hair. Her head tossed, her hips shook. When his tongue speared into her, she cried out in a strangled whisper. Her panting grew louder, until she puffed like a bellows gone amok.

And still Fargo did not let up. He drank his fill of her sugary juices, his chin becoming slick with the overflow. She helped matters by clamping her hands on the back of his head and mashing his face into her womanhood. Her cries increased in tempo, if not in volume. Especially when he slid a finger into her crack and pumped it in and out. She trembled. She sobbed. She did not seem to want him to ever stop.

Fargo licked until his tongue grew sore and he had to break for air. Resting his chin on her bush, he wrapped his hands around her breasts. Her red lips fell open and a heartfelt sigh escaped them. He kissed her stomach, pausing to dip his tongue into her navel. She was aflame with wanton craving, her body molten, a two-legged volcano about to blow.

And she was not the only one. Fargo unbuckled his belt and

pushed his buckskin pants down around his knees. His pole sprang free, poised to lance into her. She delighted him by taking it in her hand and gently rubbing. Their mouths fused again, and this time stayed fused.

Fargo endured her caresses as long as he dared. When a tingle warned that he was close to exploding, he pried her fingers off, dipped at the knees, touched the tip of his shaft to her sheath, and in a bold, powerful thrust, buried himself to the hilt.

The redhead humped up off the ground, lifting him clear into the air. Her fingernails raked his arms. Her legs closed around his waist, locking him there, while a catty grin curled her luscious lips.

Fargo grasped her hips and bunched his stomach muscles. He commenced stroking her, settling into a smooth, easy rhythm that would bring them to the brink slowly. Dorette did not try to rush him, as some women might have. She was content to let him do as he pleased at the pace he pleased, which added to his pleasure. Rocking on his knees, he soon had her thrashing and groaning and aquiver with anticipation.

A knot formed at the base of Fargo's manhood. His throat grew constricted. His organ swelled. The signs were all there. He was on the verge. All he could do now was hold onto her and let their mutual release build to its inevitable climax. As if she sensed the same thing, she clasped him close and hiked her bottom to better accommodate him.

"I'm ready!" Dorette whispered.

That was all it took. Those two simple words triggered Fargo's pent-up urge to explode. His whole frame shook with the intensity of his release as he slammed into her hard enough to lift her off the ground. Uttering short moans, she clung to him, lost in a delirium of her own. Their bodies slapped in steady cadence. Together, they surged to the summit. Together, they crested, Fargo oblivious to all else except the writhing form under him.

It took forever for Fargo to coast to a stop. Spent and weary, he collapsed on top of her, his chest cushioned by her yielding globes. Her fingers toyed with his hair and traced the edge of his ear.

"That was nice," Dorette said dreamily.

Fargo merely grunted.

"We'll have to do it again sometime."

Fargo wondered if she was one of those women who expected a second helping minutes after the first. Given all he had been through that day, he was too tired to please her a second time so soon.

The wind gusted, stirring Fargo's hair, chilling his back. Temperature extremes in the desert never failed to amaze him. In twelve hours he would be roasting, but at the moment he was actually cold. He snuggled closer to Dorette, who wrapped her arms around his shoulders. Her body radiated warmth like a fire.

It was quite some time before Fargo roused himself and rolled off. He dressed quickly. She followed suit, her movements sluggish.

"Maybe I'll take you up on that offer of some sleep," Dorette said. "My eyelids feel as if they weigh a ton."

Fargo figured that she would climb from their roost and go lie down with her sister. Instead, she clutched her rifle, curled into a ball right there, and was out to the world within moments. He moved to the end of the shelf nearest the mouth of the draw, the Henry tucked against his side, and leaned his head back.

By all rights, Fargo should be exhausted. He had not had a moment's rest since daybreak. Yet his mind refused to slow down. He could not stop thinking of Veronica Langtree and the Gantrys. He could not help plotting how best to elude Trench and the other gunmen once the sun rose. He was sure they were still out there, biding their time, awaiting first light.

The hours passed calmly. Finally Fargo grew drowsy and had to fight to stay awake. By the position of the constellations he knew when midnight arrived. Still, he made no move to awaken the redhead until he was so tired that his mind felt like mush.

Dorette did not snap to her feet right away. She mumbled and protested, muttering to be left alone. Fargo had to shake her hard a number of times, then prop her up. She managed a wan grin.

"You're cruel, do you know that?"

"We agreed to take turns," Fargo reminded her. "You sit tight while I go check on Ava."

While he was at it, Fargo decided to scour the immediate area. First he ventured from their sanctuary. The field of boulders lay as still as a cemetery. No alien sounds carried to his ears. No fires were visible. As he turned to reenter the draw, a faint clink intruded on the tranquil scene. As best as Fargo could ascertain, it came from the direction of the bluff. If so, the pack of killers was a lot closer than he had bargained on.

Hastening up the draw, Fargo hunkered beside Ava. She slept soundly, so soundly that she never stirred when he placed a hand on her forehead. Just as Dorette had claimed, there was no fever.

All the horses were dozing. Only the Ovaro was still upright. The sorrel snorted when Fargo touched its front leg and would have risen had he not held onto the picket rope and spoken soothingly. After it quieted, he inspected the infected leg carefully. His worst fear was confirmed. The limb was so swollen that Ava would not be able to ride the animal.

Helping himself to two pieces of pemmican, Fargo went back to the shelf.

Dorette had collected a handful of pebbles and was arranging them in various patterns in front of her. "It helps me stay awake," she explained at his quizzical look. She accepted a piece of pemmican gratefully. "How much of this stuff do you have left?"

"Not near enough," Fargo said. By limiting themselves to a piece a day, it would last a week. He also had a small amount of jerky in a leather pouch, to be eaten only as a last resort.

"Shouldn't you be getting some rest?" Dorette asked.

Fargo did not need an engraved invitation. Spreading out on his back, he covered his eyes with a forearm.

"Any special time you want me to wake you?"

"No need," Fargo said. Years of getting up at the crack of dawn had made it a habit. Now, no matter how late he turned in, he always awoke as the eastern sky began to brighten. Sooner, if he put his mind to it. This morning was no exception. A full hour before sunrise he was on his feet again.

Dorette had been playing with her pebbles. She jumped when he snapped erect, then declared, "Damn! Don't do that to a person. You about gave me a conniption."

"We're leaving," Fargo announced, stepping to the edge. Every minute was critical if they were to get underway before Trench and the other gunmen began hunting for them. But as he lifted a leg to jump a boulder, the redhead's arms enclosed his waist and her lips brushed the back of his neck.

"What's your hurry, big man? It's still early yet. Ava won't wake up for hours." Dorette licked his ear. "Why don't we start the new day off on the right foot?"

Give a woman an inch, Fargo reflected, and pried loose. "Langtree's men are close by," he revealed. "We need to get the jump on them or we risk being trapped in here."

Dorette's fine spirits evaporated. "Why didn't you say so sooner?" She scooped up her rifle. "Just tell me what you want me to do and I'll do it."

The redhead was as good as her word. While Fargo saddled the Ovaro and her bay, Dorette roused Ava. They walked all three horses to the end of the draw. Fargo cupped a hand so Ava could climb on, and Dorette swung up behind her. Holding the bareback sorrel's reins, Fargo forked leather. The stars had not yet given way to the sun, but it would not be long.

Since the bluff lay to the northeast, Fargo angled to the northwest, threading his way with care among the boulders. He held to a walk so they would not make much noise. The sorrel limped badly but kept up. The sky grew pale. Stars blinked out as the light spread. Stray shafts of sunlight heralded the new day.

There was no trace of the gunmen. Fargo was congratulating himself on having outwitted them when a pair of gunshots rocked the wasteland due north of their position. He promptly reined up. From near the bluff came two more shots. Then, east of it, two more.

"What do you reckon that was all about?" Ava wondered.

"Signals," Dorette whispered.

Fargo was inclined to agree. The gunmen had spread out and were seeking sign of them. It was time to put the ruse he had in mind into effect. Climbing down, he looped a twelve-foot length of rope around the sorrel's neck. To the end he tied a small, rectangular rock. Pointing the sorrel eastward, he removed his hat and slapped it on the animal's rump. The horse limped briskly off, dragging the rock. As he had intended, it raised a cloud of dust in the process.

Vaulting onto the pinto, Fargo stuck to their original course. He hugged the shadows, the gullies, and the draws. They had not gone very far when from the vicinity of the bluff three shots rang out. They were answered by single shots to the west and the east. If Fargo was right, it meant that a lookout at the bluff had spotted the dust cloud and signaled for the rest to close in.

In that case, the way ahead should be clear.

Fargo was taking no chances, though. He rode with the Henry across his thighs, availing himself of every bit of cover, just as an Apache would. Where there was none, he crossed quickly, then covered the women while they did likewise. Soon they were west of the bluff. They came on a line of tracks made by a lone rider. Fresh tracks, left not long ago. The hoofprints led off toward the dust raised by the sorrel.

Fargo could not help but grin. He had done it. Now he was behind the gunmen, with nothing ahead save empty country. By noon the women would be safe in the mountains.

Then a low ridge loomed before them. Rather than go around, Fargo climbed to scan the countryside. The slope was hard-packed, littered with talus. Rocks and stones rolled out from under the Ovaro and rattled to the bottom. He did not mean to make much noise. It simply could not be helped.

Near the top, Fargo had to jump a cleft. His attention was on the ground, where it should not be. Consequently, he had no idea someone had popped up above him until a flinty voice barked, "Hold it right here, mister! Or else!"

There were two of them, hard cases Fargo had never set eyes on before, one with a rifle, the other holding a Remington six-shooter. They had him dead to rights. The only reason he could think of for their not opening fire immediately was that Langtree had given orders to take him alive.

The Ovaro partially blocked their view of the bay, which worked in his favor. For no sooner were the words out of the rifleman's mouth than Dorette Gantry's Spencer cracked and the man's shoulder erupted in a scarlet spray. He toppled. The partner fanned the Remington, rushing his shots as he flung himself backward. He missed all three times.

In a twinkling, Fargo wheeled the stallion and raced for a cluster of boulders at the bottom. The sisters had the same idea, but their bay, burdened by their combined weight, was not as quick to respond. They were well short of the bottom when the gunman with the Remington popped up again and sent more lead after them.

Fargo had the Henry elevated, and when the hard case rose, he fired. The slug chipped stone slivers off the top of the ridge, driving the man to cover. It bought them the time needed to reach the boulders.

"Now what?" Ava asked once they were temporarily safe. "Every last one of those varmints knows where we are now."

Langtree's cutthroats had them boxed in on three sides. Once again the only way out was to the south. And once again, Fargo hesitated. They didn't stand a snowball's chance in hell of outrunning the hired guns. Not unless they could get their hands on another horse.

"Well?" Dorette goaded.

"Stick close," Fargo directed, winding southward in spite of his reservations.

Ava flapped her legs against the bay. "Where did those last two gun sharks come from?" she wanted to know. "I thought we had them all hoodwinked."

Fargo wondered about the same thing. He was sure the pair on the ridge had not been with Trench the day before. Yet if that was the case, then more gunnies had shown up during the night. From where? And how many? Did the blond have a small army at her beck and call? Had there been more than one pack of killers scouring the Sierra for Gantry?

A flurry of shots from the ridge reminded Fargo that there was a time and a place for everything, and at the moment he had better concentrate on staying alive. The questions could wait.

Once they were out of the boulders, a winding gulch led them to a narrow, barren plain bordered in the distance by a low, stark volcanic escarpment, half butte, half mountain, carved by the whimsical hand of Nature eons ago. It was the nearest haven, so without delay Fargo goaded the women on and glued the Ovaro to the bay's tail.

A great bloated toad of a sun sat on the rim of the earth. The night's welcome chill was no more. In the span of half an hour the temperature had climbed twenty degrees, hinting at the worse heat to come before the day was done.

Fargo constantly twisted in the saddle. Scattered signal shots confirmed the gunmen were converging and would soon give chase. Somehow, he had to shake them, a near-impossible task with a wounded woman and an overburdened mount on his hands. Plus there was the little matter of their tracks, sign so fresh that a five-year-old could shadow them with no problem at all. Unless their mounts sprouted wings, their own trail would lead Trench right to them.

Over three-quarters of the plain had been covered when Fargo looked back for the tenth or eleventh time. Riders spilled from a gorge to the northwest. Others appeared at the top of a knoll. Combined, there had to be fifteen, maybe more. And prominent among those on the knoll was a slender figure whose long blond hair shimmered like the sun. The lady herself had arrived.

"That bitch!" Ava hissed. "Where did she come from?"

The two groups swept out onto the plain, merging into one body with Veronica Langtree at its head.

Fargo studied the upthrust volcanic rock in front of them. A switchback connected to a spur halfway up. No one would be able to get at them, on that side at least, without riding straight into his gun sights. Assuming the lead, he flew up the escarpment, the big stallion responding smoothly to the slightest pressure of the reins. He leaped off before the pinto stopped, sank to one knee on the rim, and sighted down the barrel.

Just then Veronica Langtree raised a hand, bringing her pack of human wolves to a halt well out of range. A parlay was held. One of the men could be seen rummaging in his saddlebags.

Ava and Dorette had taken up positions on either side of Fargo. The redhead patted her Spencer, saying, "All I ask is one clear shot at her, Lord. One measly shot."

"Wait your turn," Ava said. "I'm the one she bushwhacked."

Fargo didn't take his eyes off the activity below. A white shirt was produced and tied to the muzzle of a rifle barrel. The rifle, in turn, was handed to Veronica, who boldly flourished it and advanced.

"Look at her!" Dorette declared. "Does she really think that we'll honor a white flag?" The redhead raised the Spencer.

Fargo was not about to interfere. With the blonde dead, the others might give up. Then two figures on horseback were ushered to the front of the pack. Both had been bound. Several guns were pointed at each of them. That far off, their faces were pale blurs. But Fargo did not need to see their features to identify them.

It was Luke and Willa Gantry.

9

"Pa! Sis!" Ava Gantry cried. Leaping erect, she bolted toward the bottom.

Skye Fargo caught her in three strides. She tried to wrench free but he would not permit it. "Go down there and you'll either be shot or trussed up like they are."

"No! Let me go, damn you!" Ava had partially regained the use of her wounded arm. She swung her rifle at his temple, missed, and drew it back to try again.

Dorette rushed over, grabbing the barrel and whispering firmly, "Calm down! He's right and you know it. We have to wait and see what the blond witch wants before we do anything."

Fargo let the redhead deal with the youngest sister while he returned to his vantage point. Veronica Langtree betrayed no fear as she crossed the baked plain. As relaxed as if she were on her way to a church social, she ascended the butte, not reining up until she was a mere fifteen feet away. The barbed looks bestowed on her by the sisters only made her grin. To Fargo she bobbed her chin and said, "Nice to see you again, big man. But I can't say as much for the company you keep."

Ava bristled, whipping her rifle up. "You bitch! Insult us again and I'll blow your damn brains out!"

Veronica was not the least bit afraid. "I don't think so. Because if you harm a hair on my head, my men have orders to fill your precious father and sister full of holes. So behave yourself, little girl."

Outraged, Ava took a step, but had the presence of mind to

stop when Dorette blocked her path. Ava shook a fist, saying, "You wait, woman! You'll get your due someday!"

"But not today," Veronica said flatly. Shifting her attention to Fargo, she went on. "Since I can trust you to keep your head, I'll deal directly with you instead of these hicks. I don't know what your connection is to Luke Gantry. Frankly, I don't even care. All that matters to me is finding where he struck the vein."

"You don't know yet?" Fargo said.

Veronica gave an angry toss of her golden mane. "They won't talk. I've tried to persuade them to be reasonable. I even offered to let them keep some of the gold. But they're both as stubborn as mules."

Fargo didn't blame them. Luke Gantry was a gold-blind fool, but not a complete idiot. Langtree had no intention of letting any of them live once she knew the secret.

"Here's what I have in mind," she went on. "A trade. Their lives for the gold. Tell me where it is, and once I confirm it, I'll release Luke and Willa."

Ava snorted in contempt. "Do you honestly expect us to trust you?"

"No," Veronica admitted frankly. "But I do expect you to care whether your precious pa and that worthless sister of yours go on breathing." Smirking, she leaned forward. "To help you make the right decision, here's something you should know. We had to chase them halfway to the Amargosa before we were able to catch them, and then only because a lucky shot dropped your father's horse right out from under him. We surrounded them and I asked them to give up. Being the jackasses they are, they refused. When the shooting was over, I had lost a good man and they had both taken bullets."

Ava was aghast at the news. "They've been shot?"

Veronica nodded. "Willa caught one in the shoulder, your pa in the chest. Both have lost a lot of blood. They need doctoring, but they won't get any from me." Her sinister smile widened. "Think of it as incentive. Tell me where you struck gold. Once I make sure you're not lying, I'll turn them over to you so you can tend them. That's as fair as I can be."

Dorette and Ava were too upset to comment.

"There's no hurry in making up your minds," Veronica said. "I'll give you an hour to talk it over." Winking at Fargo, she turned and descended the switchback at a leisurely pace, sitting straight and brazen in the saddle.

"The gall of that woman," Dorette muttered.

Fargo eased the hammer on the Henry down and took a seat under a rock overhang. Whatever happened next was out of his hands. If the sisters wanted to trade the information for the lives of Luke and Willa, that was their business.

For half an hour Dorette and Ava debated the right thing to do. Neither of them believed Langtree would honor her pledge to release Luke and Willa even if they gave precise directions to the gorge, and they were at a loss to think of another way to free their father and sister from the blonde's clutches without doing so. Finally, exasperated, they walked to the overhang.

"What do we do?" Ava asked outright.

"We need your advice," Dorette whispered.

Fargo had his hat pulled low over his eyes and had been resting. Sitting up, he regarded them for a moment. "I have to be honest with you," he said. "I don't care whether your father and Willa live or die."

Dorette swallowed hard. "I suppose we can't blame you, not after how you were treated. But we need your help anyway. Please. For my sake, if for no other reason."

Ava gave Fargo a barbed glance, which he pretended not to notice. "The way I see it," he began, "Langtree has you over a barrel. Luke and Willa will die if you don't tell her what she wants to know. It's as simple as that."

"They'll die anyway," Ava said.

"Maybe not," Fargo responded. "She's not the only one who can make conditions. Tell her that you'll draw her a map. Tell her that she can go see for herself that the gold is there. But first she has to hand over your father and sister to you."

Dorette was skeptical. "Langtree would never agree to those terms. She'd be afraid we'd light a shuck and she'd be left holding a worthless map."

"She can leave most of her men here to make sure we don't

go anywhere before she gets back," Fargo suggested. "That way, you get to tend your father and sister, and we gain time to come up with a way to escape."

"We're grasping at straws," Ava said.

Dorette motioned sharply. "What else can we do? She just might go for Skye's plan. She has little to lose and everything to gain if she learns where the pit is."

"If it doesn't work, we're no worse off than we are now," Fargo said. He did not mention that he had another plan to fall back on in the event the first one fell through. They would want to hear the details, and they wouldn't like them one bit.

Ava took to pacing. Dorette sulked. The heat was stifling. Not a single cloud marred the blue vault above them. The volcanic rock grew hot to the touch, except where there was shade, and even there it was uncomfortably warm. Fargo rationed a few sips of water to each of them and filled his hat for each horse.

"Here she comes," Ava announced presently.

Waving the rifle with the white shirt attached, Veronica Langtree trotted up to the spur. She smiled broadly, confident she had the upper hand. Drawing rein, she forked a long leg around her saddle horn. "Well? What will it be?"

"We've made up our minds," Ava said.

Veronica nodded. "I knew you'd make the right choice. So let's get this over with."

"Not so fast," Ava responded. "We're going to do this our way or not at all."

"Your way?"

While Ava outlined the terms Fargo had suggested, he stepped to the rim. The gunmen had dismounted. Trench and Otis were huddled in conversation. Several others lounged on the ground. Only a few held guns fixed on the Gantrys. One of them was the skinny kid with the bowler hat, Crespin. Acting nonchalant, Fargo began to drift toward Veronica Langtree's big roan just as the blonde uttered a string of oaths.

"Who do you think you are," she railed at Ava, "dictating conditions to me? I should have known better than to think I could reason with a bunch of yahoos." She voiced more lusty curses. "No, I won't trade your father and sister for a map. No, I won't leave them here with you while I go off on a wild-goose chase. We do things my way or not at all."

Ava did not let Langtree intimidate her. "Not if you want to get your hands on the gold, we don't. We're not as dumb as you'd like to think, lady. You might have Pa and Willa in your power, but you'll never get your hands on the gold if you harm them."

Fargo sidled nearer, switching the Henry from his right hand to his left.

"Think so, do you, little one?" Veronica snarled. "Well, here's where I prove you wrong. Let's see if you're still so cocky after you see your sister gunned down right before your eyes."

"You wouldn't!" Ava said.

Veronica, her features the perfect picture of pure evil, raised a hand to signal. It was just as Fargo had foreseen. Langtree was not about to back down. The moment had come to put his other plan into effect. Darting to the roan, he grabbed Langtree by the front of her expensive blouse and threw her to the ground. Dazed, she clawed under her short riding jacket, but he batted her hand aside with the Henry and stooped to snatch a short-barreled Colt from a small holster on her right hip. From the plain rose harsh shouts as Fargo roughly hauled her to her feet.

Ava and Dorette were too stunned to move. The redhead came alive when Fargo tossed the Henry to her. "What in the world do you think you're doing?"

"Don't interfere," Fargo said. Shoving the blonde to the edge of the switchback, he pressed her own pistol against her head. Below, the gunmen were scrambling for their horses. Otis had already mounted and was flying like a madman toward the escarpment.

Langtree was caked with dust, her hair mussed. Glaring at him out of the corner of her eyes, she snarled, "No one man-handles me, big man. You'll pay for this."

"I'd be quiet if I were you," Fargo said, "unless you can fly." To press home his point, he gave her a short push. She teetered on the brink and would have pitched over the side had he not yanked her back.

Otis reached the switchback in no time, his arms out from his sides to show he was not holding a gun. He reined up when Fargo gestured, and yelled, "We'll do whatever you want, mister! Just don't hurt her!"

Trench and five or six others were galloping to the rescue. "Make them stop!" Fargo commanded, gouging the Colt into Veronica to make her wince.

"You think you're so damn smart," she snapped. "How did you figure it out?"

Fargo did not know what she meant and had no time to question her. The grizzled frontiersman had faced the onrushing killers and was frantically motioning for them to halt.

"Go back! Go back! She won't be harmed so long as we do as he wants!"

Trench and the others slowed.

"Are you all hard of hearin'?" Otis practically screamed. "Stop right there, you jackasses! So help me, the man who doesn't listen will wish he'd never been born! That includes you, Trench! I know how you feel, but back off until I see what he wants."

Dorette and Ava had stepped to the brink. The redhead shook her head in amazement as the six gun sharks wheeled their animals and rode back to join those guarding her kin. "You did it!" she whispered. "I never would have thought it would be this easy."

"Don't kid yourself," Veronica spat. "He only thinks he has the upper hand."

Fargo swung her around so that she was between Otis and them. The old-timer made no attempt to come any closer. "This is how we'll do it," he declared. "You send Luke and Willa up. When they're halfway, I'll let Veronica start down. Ava and Dorette will be covering her every step of the way, so no tricks."

The blonde was sizzling, and not from the heat. "Don't do it, Otis! I don't care what they do to me. You're not to swap. Savvy?"

"I won't let any harm come to you," Otis said.

"He's bluffing," Veronica said smugly. "Just like he did the first time we tangled. He doesn't have what it takes to shove me to my death."

Ava jabbed the blonde in the back. "Maybe Fargo doesn't, but I sure as hell do. Send my pa and my sister up to us or they'll be scraping you off the ground with a knife."

Otis overheard. "I'm going, missy. Just hold your horses. And remember, no tricks at your end, either. We'll have your pappy and that loudmouthed shrew covered every step of the way." Lashing his reins, he hastened off.

Fargo lowered the Colt. It was a .36-caliber Navy, the barrel sawed off close to the cylinder, the trigger guard removed to grant quicker access to the trigger. A typical gambler's gun. He tucked it under his wide brown leather belt and reclaimed the Henry.

Langtree studied him as if he were a bug she wanted to smash. "Don't think you've beaten me, mister, because you haven't. All you're doing is delaying the inevitable. Eventually I'll learn where their diggings are located."

"Some people are never satisfied," Fargo remarked.

"What does that mean?"

"You already own one of the finest gambling halls in southern California. You make more money in a month that most people make in a year. You can afford a nice house, the best clothes, whatever else you want. Yet that's not enough. You need to have more."

The blonde was amused. "There's no such thing as having enough money, big man. The more a person has, the more they want. And not because of what money can buy." She paused. "No, the real value of money is in the power it gives you. The power to influence others. The power to do as you please without being accountable to anyone. Politicians know that. It's the key to success."

"By whose standard?" Fargo countered. He had heard it all before. Those who had a lot were always lording it over anyone who had less. In her own way, Veronica Langtree was as much a slave of her greed as Luke Gantry was of his.

"Wouldn't you like to be rich?" the blonde asked.

"I've never given it much thought," Fargo said honestly.

"Then you're as dull-witted as the Gantry clan. Anyone content to go through life with empty pockets has no idea what living is all about."

Fargo was not going to debate the point. He knew that she was wrong, and he also knew that he could talk until he was blue in the face and it wouldn't change her opinion. Some people believed only what they wanted to believe.

An argument had broken out on the plain. Otis and Trench were embroiled in a shouting match. The gist was not hard to follow. Trench refused to let the prospector and Willa climb the escarpment. Otis insisted that they were going to, whether Trench liked the idea or not. And it was the tall gunman who backed down.

Which surprised Fargo. He'd had the impression that Trench was Langtree's top man. Yet it was the crusty frontiersman who barked commands, who had men pulling rifles from scabbards and fanning out, and who led Luke and Willa forward.

"Damn him," Veronica growled. "He never listens. I don't know why I've put up with him as long as I have. If I had any sense, I'd let Trench put windows in his skull."

"He's saving your life," Ava noted. "That should count for something."

"The only thing that counts is doing as he's told," Veronica said. "When this is over, I think I'll have him horsewhipped for not listening. I did it once before when he bucked me. Just because he's my father, he thinks he can fuss over me as he sees fit."

Fargo and the sisters swung around, unable to hide their surprise.

Dorette was horrified. "You had your own pa whipped?" she whispered.

Veronica was watching her men. "I've done the same to others. Anyone who works for me has to do as I tell them to do or suffer the consequences."

"But your own *pa*?" Dorette said.

The blonde noticed their expressions. "Why do all of you look so shocked? He's still alive, isn't he?"

By then Otis and the Gantrys were near the switchback. They halted. Farther out, Trench and the hired guns had formed a half-circle facing the spur, each and every man with a rifle tucked to a shoulder. At the first hint of treachery, they would unleash a withering volley.

Otis stood in the stirrups. "We're ready at this end, mister," he hollered. "Do they walk or ride?"

"Ride," Fargo answered, since they needed the horses. As Luke Gantry and Willa started up, he steered Veronica to the roan and had her climb on. Wisely, he held the bridle to prevent her from leaving before he was ready. She glared at everyone and everything, her rosy lips twitching in repressed fury.

Ava stepped closer to the first turn, a vantage point that gave her a clear view to the bottom. Smiling sweetly at the blonde, she said, "Now remember. We'll have our sights on you until you're out of range."

"Every dog has its day," Veronica growled. "Enjoy yours while you can. My turn will come sooner than you think."

Luke and Willa climbed slowly, since they had to guide their horses with their legs alone. Luke glanced back often, as if in dread of a slug in the back. Willa appeared mad, as usual. Neither had a gunshot wound; the blonde had lied.

When the Gantrys reached the halfway point, Fargo gave the roan a light slap. "It was nice seeing you again, Miss Langtree," he could not resist taunting her. "Be sure and go slow until you're at the bottom. We wouldn't want to shoot you by mistake."

Dorette aimed her rifle at the blonde's back. "If I shoot her, Skye, it won't be an accident."

The vicious gleam in Veronica's cold eyes warned Fargo that she was close to the breaking point. He observed her closely as she walked the roan to the nearest bend, passing Ava along the way. Once around it, she glanced toward Trench. Fargo could not see her face, but she did not appear to signal the tall killer in any way.

The switchback was barely wide enough for two horses moving abreast, certainly not for three. Veronica reined to the right, close to the wall, and sat there while Luke and Willa filed past. Luke leered. Willa tried to spit on Veronica but missed and hit the roan. Blazing hatred was reflected in the scathing glance the blonde shot at them. Then she rode on.

"Pa!" Ava called, waving.

"Another sixty feet and the pair would reach the spur. Fargo shifted to better see Langtree, who had moved to the middle of the switchback and partly twisted in the saddle. She was up to something. He was sure of it. But what it might be, he couldn't guess.

Veronica reached the second turn. She raised a hand, seemingly to run it through her hair. Her real intent became clear when she suddenly swung onto the far side of her mount, Indian fashion, and clung on with one arm and leg while urging the roan into a gallop. At the same time, at the top of her lungs, she screeched, "Now, Trench! Now!"

At a command from the tall killer, the bloodthirsty pack blazed away, fifteen rifles booming in unison.

Fargo leaped for the Ovaro as slugs whistled all around him, zinging off rocks at his feet and rocks above. Grasping the bridle, he pulled the stallion back as far as it could go. The bay, left to fend for itself, took a bullet high in the shoulder and whinnied in terror. Dorette had dropped into a crouch and was returning fire, while Ava sped to help her father and Willa.

Veronica Langtree was in full flight down the escarpment.

Fargo knew that Luke and Willa would never reach safety without his help, yet helping those two was the last thing he wanted to do. Ava and Dorette, however, had stood by him, had gone against the wishes of their own father to save him. So, for their sake, he dashed to the redhead's side and added his Henry to the din. His first shot hurled a gunman to the earth. His second shattered another's shoulder. His third clipped a hard case in the thigh.

Luke and Willa had bent low. Ava reached them, scooped up their reins, and pulled their mounts toward the Ovaro.

Dorette was firing just as fast as she could work her rifle. In her eagerness to protect her family, she missed most of her targets.

"Take your time!" Fargo advised, pumping the Henry's lever to feed another bullet into the chamber.

Otis had joined in the battle. He was banging away at Luke Gantry, but the angle prevented him from getting a clear shot. When his daughter reached the bottom and streaked on by him without saying a word, he retreated, covering her.

Fargo settled his sights on Veronica's horse. He did not make a habit of shooting women, but he could not let her get away. To his amazement, she jerked upright and hauled on the reins, sliding to a stop less than twenty yards out. It was a perfect shot. He couldn't possibly miss. Then he saw her look both ways in consternation. His finger on the trigger, he did the same, and could not believe his eyes.

For pouring out onto the plain from the east and west streamed a horde of painted Mohave warriors.

10

The blast of rifles made a deafening din. Booming retort after booming retort blended into continuous thunder. Thunder so loud that at first the pack of hired killers did not hear the war whoops of the Mohaves. Not until Veronica Langtree pointed and screamed shrill warnings did a few of them turn and see the charging ranks of deadly warriors. Trench's deep voice roared above the gunfire, alerting the rest.

Lead stopped whistling off the volcanic rock on the spur. Skye Fargo straightened as the gunmen whirled to confront their new enemy. Fargo did not even try to count the Mohaves; there were too many, making the outcome a foregone conclusion.

The gunmen opened fire on the foremost warriors, who were armed with clubs, lances, and bows. Only the archers were in close enough range to use their weapons, and they had to let their shafts fly while on the run. Most missed.

At the initial volley over a dozen Mohaves went down. But those behind simply bounded over them and kept on going. Another volley dropped many more. But it was apparent that there were nowhere near enough gunmen to stop the shrieking swarm.

"We have to get out of here," Fargo declared. "The Mohaves will be after us next."

Luke and Willa had reached the top. Ava had cut her father loose and was doing the same for her older sister.

"You have some explaining to do, sissy," Willa was saying. "You're supposed to be back at the gorge. How did the three of you get here? And why the hell isn't Fargo wearing his leg irons?"

Ava finished slicing and stepped back. "I won't lie to you. We set him free."

"You did what?" Luke bellowed. "I ought to tan your hides! Since when do you decide what to do? I'm head of this family, and what I say goes."

Fargo swung onto the Ovaro and turned the stallion toward the summit. "Save your breath for riding," he said as he started up. There was no trail to the top. They would have to pick their way with care and hope that once they reached the crest they found a way down the other side.

Dorette had dashed to her bay but had not climbed on. Blood poured from the bullet hole in its shoulder, and it was doubtful the animal would last a mile. "Pa," she said, "Ava and I need to ride double with Willa and you."

"Like hell," Luke rasped. "You're both turncoats. The two of you can walk, for all I care. And if those savages get you, it will serve you right for disobeying me."

Fargo almost shot the man then and there. Sighting down the Henry, he said, "You'll let them ride with you or you'll be the ones walking."

Down on the plain, four gunmen transfixed by arrows lay on the ground, one convulsing, another wildly flapping his arms. Two others had shafts sticking from their bodies but were still in the saddle. Trench barked orders, keeping the rest spaced out in a line rather than letting them bunch up and be picked off more easily. They made for the escarpment, working their rifles nonstop, dropping Mohaves right and left. But for every warrior that fell, three more were there to take his place. And some of the Mohaves were now close enough to let their lances fly. A horse went down, whinnying stridently, pierced in the neck.

Luke Gantry looked as if he were going to give Fargo a hard time until he heard the stricken mount. Glancing at the frenzied battle, he swore, then reluctantly offered his hand to Ava. Dorette climbed up behind Willa.

Fargo did not like having the prospector at his back, but he doubted Luke would try anything until they were in the clear.

Goading the pinto up and over a jagged spine, he went around a large stone bubble and up a narrow cleft to a ledge.

Langtree's men had reached the switchback, four or five more having fallen along the way. The remainder fought on as men possessed, their blistering gunfire slowing the Mohaves, who showered arrows and lances down on them. Otis stayed beside Veronica, shooting any warrior who posed a threat.

Fargo went on. The narrow ledge wound upward across the face of the escarpment to a ramp of pockmarked rock that gave them the means of reaching a flat crown just below the summit.

"I hope to hell you know what you're doing," Luke groused. "We could end up trapped."

"You can always go back down," Fargo said to shut the man up. Moving onto a wide knob, he climbed to the highest point on the butte. A single misstep on the stallion's part would send him plunging hundreds of feet to his death on the huge boulders below. He reined up.

Fargo's gamble had paid off. The south face of the escarpment was a steep slope broken by a gully near the bottom. Leaning back and swinging the stirrups forward, he jabbed his spurs and started down. Dirt and dust spewed out from under the Ovaro as the big horse slid a dozen feet before it could dig in its hooves for purchase. Fargo slanted to the left to miss a boulder. Below it the ground grew firmer.

A glance showed the Gantrys poised at the summit. Willa and Luke did not have as much confidence in their mounts as he did in the pinto. They edged onto the slope slowly, their animals shoulder to shoulder.

On the sluggish breeze wafted the fierce war whoops of the Mohaves, punctuated by the constant crash of rifles and pistols. So far the gunmen were holding their own, but it would not be long before they were overwhelmed.

Fargo avoided a sinkhole. He came to a section of slope littered with gravel and angled past it. The sun baked him alive. His soaked buckskins clung to his limbs. It would have been nice to shed his shirt, if not for the risk of having his skin fried. In the gully he found some shade, but not enough to offer relief.

Reaching the bottom well ahead of the Gantrys, Fargo halted. They were not even halfway down, Willa slightly in the lead. Instead of following the safe path he had picked, they had blundered onto the gravel slope. Loose stones clattered down with every step their mounts took.

To the north the gunfire had abruptly ended. The cries of the Mohaves had dwindled. Fargo hoped the Indians were too busy taking care of their wounded and stripping the bodies of the gunmen to come after the Gantrys and him.

To the south stretched a limitless expanse of desert. For as far as the eye could see not a single plant grew, not so much as a solitary weed or dry shrub or stunted tree. Nothing moved out there. It was a dead land. A harsh land that bred hard men. A land as hostile to human life as the Mohaves were hostile to those who dared trespass in it.

A squeal lifted Fargo's gaze to the slopes above. Luke's horse had stumbled and was tottering toward Willa's. She tried to rein aside, but her own animal could not keep its footing on the gravel and slipped. The prospector swore lustily as his mount collided with hers. Both horses crashed down, spilling their riders, sending all four of them tumbling.

Fargo was helpless to do more than watch as Ava and Dorette rolled and slid for over fifty feet, to the brink of the gully. The redhead favored her left leg when she rose. Ava pressed a hand to her bandage. They had to spring to safety when Willa's animal hurtled toward them in a spray of dust and stones. It slid to a stop on an incline and thrashed its legs, unable to rise until Dorette grabbed the reins and pulled.

It was a wonder none of them broke an arm or leg. Luke was caked with dirt and mad enough to spit nails. When he caught up to his animal, he bit it across the head several times with his open hand. Willa was strangely quiet.

They walked the horses into the gully, mounted, and were soon at Fargo's side. He was glad the water skin hung from his saddle and not one of theirs, or they might have lost all their precious water. Without saying a word, he reined the stallion to the west. His idea was to loop wide around the escarpment and head for the Sierra Nevada.

Fargo had traveled a short distance when he spotted figures flitting among the boulders to the northwest. Instantly, he halted. There were six or seven, maybe more, bounding like bronzed antelope toward him. Mohaves. And several held bows.

"Head south!" Fargo shouted, and did just that, lashing the reins to bring the stallion to a gallop. A shaft whizzed past his left shoulder. Another almost clipped the pinto. He snapped off a couple of shots to discourage pursuit.

A boulder the size of a log cabin reared in front of him. Fargo veered to the right as more feathered shafts struck on all sides. One hit the pommel of his saddle and glanced off, nicking his shin. Then the boulder was behind him, screening him. Flat land opened ahead so he gave the stallion its head.

The Gantrys galloped around the other side of the boulder, Dorette firing at the warriors. She stopped after a bit and held on tight to Luke as her father needlessly whipped their horse.

Fargo outdistanced the Mohaves rapidly. It was a small group—latecomers, he reckoned, who had not arrived in time for the battle. The sheer number of the war party convinced him there had to be a village nearby, and the last thing he wanted to do was stumble upon it. He kept his eyes peeled for sign as he neared another rock outcropping, this one much smaller than the escarpment. Slowing, he checked on the Gantrys. They were sixty yards back, Willa still in the lead, Luke's mount caked with lather and flagging.

Ava pointed at him and yelled. Fargo didn't quite catch her words, so he shook his head. She yelled again, jabbing a finger at the stallion's rear legs. Or so he thought, until he glanced down and saw an arrow jutting from the water skin. Hauling on the reins, he stopped and sprang off. The barbed tip had pierced the hide inches from the bottom. Most of the water was already gone. He yanked the bag off and turned it upside down to save what little was left.

"Not very smart, are you, mister?" Luke declared as the

Gantrys caught up. "Didn't you think to keep an eye on it? We aren't going to last two days out here now."

Dorette climbed down. "It could have happened to anyone, Pa. It's not his fault."

"Sidin' with him now, are you?" Luke said sternly.

Fargo gave the water skin to the redhead to hold while he examined the Ovaro. He was glad to find the shaft had not gone clean through. Taking his rope, he cut a short length and tied it fast around the water skin below the hole. The arrow he broke in half and tossed to the ground.

"Hey, look!" Ava suddenly said.

The Mohaves were still after them. Strung out in single file, the warriors jogged at a steady, mile-eating pace. As yet they were not within bow range.

"Filthy heathens," Luke said.

"They'll never give up," Willa remarked.

Fargo slung the water skin onto his saddle and followed suit. A hand fell on his leg.

"Can I ride with you, Skye?" Dorette asked softly. "Please."

Her father made a sound reminiscent of a riled bear. "Skye, is it? I never thought I'd live to see the day my own flesh and blood would turn on me as you've done, girl. You've stabbed me in the back, is what you've done. I hope you're proud of your treachery."

"What we were doing to him was wrong, Pa," Dorette said.

Luke glowered at her. "Says who? You? *I'm* the head of this family. It's my right to decide what is right and what is wrong. You betrayed me, girl. You betrayed all the Gantrys who have ever lived."

"She did no such thing, Pa," Ava threw in. "You can't hold it against her for doing what she thought was best."

"Ahhh. The other traitor speaks," Luke spat. "You're just as guilty as she is, sissy. As guilty as sin, the both of you. May the good Lord forgive you for what you've done, since I sure as hell never will."

Fargo was not going to listen to any more. Bending an arm, he swung Dorette up behind him. Her arms went around his waist, her cheek on his shoulder. At a brisk walk he rode to the outcropping and on into a wash. It ran to the southeast, widening out onto another plain. Fargo lost sight of the Mohaves—and intended to keep it that way. As much as he would have liked to linger in the shadow of the outcropping, to let the horses rest, he pushed on.

Presently Dorette lifted her head and whispered, "Why did I do it, Skye? Why did I let him treat me like a cur all those years? Why did it take me so long to realize that I was wasting my life by staying with him?"

Fargo shrugged. "A friend of mine, a Sioux warrior, had a saying he was fond of. He claimed that it's not the rattlesnake on the next rise that we have to watch out for. It's the one right under our own feet."

"A Sioux said that?"

"Indians aren't stupid, Dorette, no matter what you've heard. My friend was what you might call a medicine man, and he was one of the wisest hombres I've ever run across."

"What did he have to say about getting hitched?"

The unexpected question gave Fargo pause. Her motive for asking was as plain as the twin mounds pressed hard against his back. "He liked to say that women have more ways of snaring men than men do of snaring rabbits."

The redhead chuckled. "What do you say?"

Fargo did not mince words. "That I'm not ready to settle down yet, and I doubt I will be for a long time to come. I like my freedom, Dorette. I like being able to go where I please, beholden to no one."

"That's too bad," Dorette said. "Something tells me that you would make a dandy husband."

Fargo let the subject drop. He'd learned long ago that when a woman set her sights on a man, no amount of honesty would make her change her mind. The man's only hope was to make himself mighty scarce mighty quick.

In this instance, the heat soon took their minds off everything except staying alive. It rolled off the desert floor in suffocating waves. The simple act of breathing proved difficult. Every breath seared their lungs with fire. Fargo wet his tongue and licked his lips, but they were dry before his tongue slipped back into his mouth.

"Willa is wrong, isn't she?" Dorette asked out of the blue. "The Mohaves will give up once they see that they can't catch us, won't they?"

"It depends on the Kwanamis. They're the ones in charge."

"The who?"

Fargo explained. "The Mohaves have two kinds of warriors, the Kwanamis and those who aren't Kwanamis. Those who aren't have to do whatever the Kwanamis want."

"What makes these Kwanamis so special?"

"They live for war and nothing else. They're the fighters, you might say. The warrior class. There have never been more than fifty or so in the whole tribe, but they're the ones who run things, who lead war parties and tell the rest what to do."

"I bet if my pa were a Mohave, he'd be one."

It was Fargo's turn to chuckle. The reminder made him think to check on the others. Willa and Ava plodded along a few yards behind him, while Luke Gantry, sullen and silent, brought up the rear.

The blazing sun climbed until it hung directly overhead. They had covered several miles without sign of the Mohaves, so Fargo felt safe in seeking a spot to stop. A chain of rugged outcroppings, some hundreds of feet high, others no higher than the stallion, offered plenty of places to hide. He rode deep into them and stopped in a circular basin rimmed by rock walls.

Wearily, Fargo climbed down and let the reins fall. He stepped into the shade and was about to ease to the ground when Luke Gantry reined up beside the Ovaro and reached for the water skin.

"No one drinks until I say so," Fargo said.

"Like hell." Gantry lifted the skin, shook it a few times to listen to the water slosh, then smiled eagerly and went to open it.

Fargo was not going to warn him twice. Darting over, he slammed the stock of his rifle into the prospector's stomach, doubling Gantry in half. The water skin fell from the man's numb fingers as Fargo swept the stock in an arc, brutally slugging Gantry on the jaw.

Teeth crunched. Gantry cried out and tumbled, striking on his shoulder. Hissing blood, he reared to his feet and drew back a fist.

Fargo was ready. He rammed the barrel into Gantry's gut, reversed direction, and smashed the butt into the man's cheek. The prospector staggered but was too tough to go down. Whipping a foot back, Fargo drove his boot into Gantry's groin. That did the job. Wheezing and clutching himself, Gantry melted to his knees.

"Skye! Look out!"

Dorette's cry came in the nick of time. Willa Gantry had dismounted, picked up a rock the size of a melon, and raised it on high to bash in Fargo's skull. He dodged, but could not escape a jarring blow to the shoulder. Pivoting, he did something he rarely did: He punched a woman full in the mouth. Willa crumpled near her father.

The pair glared raw spite as Fargo picked up the water skin and carried it into the shade. Sliding down, he rested the Henry across his legs.

"You bastard!" Luke Gantry said. "I'll kill you for this. Mark my words."

Ava walked to him and tenderly placed a hand on his shoulder. "You brought it on yourself, Pa. You should have listened to him. We have to ration the water. There's no telling how long it has to last us."

So mad that he shook and twitched as if about to explode, Luke smacked the hand away and thrust an accusing finger at her. "How dare you! You stood there and did nothin' while Mr. High-and-Mighty pounded on us! You let your own pa and sister be beaten bloody! And now you say it's all our fault?" Luke pushed Ava so hard she nearly fell. "Get away from me, girl! I never want you to touch me again! From this day on, I'm no longer your pa. From this day on, you're no longer my daughter. You're a Jezebel, nothin' more."

"Pa, please—" Dorette came to Ava's defense.

"The same goes for you!" Luke thundered. "Both of you can

do as you damn well please from now on. And may you rot in hell once we're out of this mess. I don't want to ever set eyes on either of you again."

"You can't mean that," Ava said.

Willa had not taken her eyes off Fargo. Crouching, she tensed, on the verge of throwing herself at him. Apparently changing her mind, she ran a hand across her mouth and licked blood from her finger. "You're to blame, mister. Until you came along, we were as close as a family could be. We hardly ever had a spat. But you changed all that. Somehow or other you've turned my sisters bad. You've set kin against kin."

Fargo made no reply. What good would it do him, he asked himself, to point out that Luke and Willa had brought the breakup of their family on themselves? Why bother pointing out that if it had not been him, someone else would have come along sooner or later, someone who treated Dorette and Ava kindly and made them see their father for the heartless bastard he was?

Ava crouched in front of Luke and extended a hand, but he batted it away again. "Tell me that you didn't mean that, Pa," she said, tears forming. "After all these years, you can't chuck us aside like you would rotten food."

"Why can't I?"

"We're your daughters!" Ava cried, clutching the front of his shirt before he could stop her. "Don't all the years you spent raising us mean anything to you?"

"No."

Ava recoiled, then balled her fists and swept them up. Dorette ran over, grabbing her arms and pulling her back. "Let me at him!" Ava screamed.

Fargo stood and moved between the prospector and the two women. "Enough," he said. "You're making too much noise. If we're not careful, the Mohaves will hear."

"Didn't you hear *him*?" Ava demanded, the tears gushing. "He's never loved us! All we've ever been to him is someone to do the cooking, someone to mend his britches, someone to clean up his messes."

Dorette ushered her younger sister thirty feet to the opposite side of the basin, where they huddled. Ava buried her face on the redhead's shoulder and bawled her heart out.

The father sneered, amused. When Ava bawled louder, he laughed.

Seldom had Fargo held so low an opinion of a man as he did of Luke Gantry. Fargo strode by him, deliberately stepping on Gantry's hand as he did. The prospector jerked his fingers back, fuming.

Going over to the water skin, Fargo pushed his hat back on his head. He cocked an ear, trying to hear above Ava's wailing. It was hopeless. The only way to make sure the Mohaves were not on the trail was for him to go see.

Fargo walked toward the gap in the wall through which they had entered. Pausing, he caught Dorette's eye, pointed at Ava, and touched a finger to his lips. The redhead gestured, in effect telling him there was nothing she could do. Peeved, he turned to the gap just as a shadow fell across it and a lanky figure materialized. Fargo tried to bring up the Henry but he was already covered.

"Howdy, sonny," Otis declared. "Did you miss us?"

Behind the grinning frontiersman stood Veronica and Trench.

11

Skye Fargo was caught flat-footed. Thanks to Ava Gantry's wailing, he had not heard their enemies approach. One twitch of Otis's trigger finger and he was a dead man. Given all that had happened, he braced for the blast he was certain would come. But Otis merely wagged the rifle to indicate he should back up. Warily, Fargo did so.

Luke Gantry spied the newcomers next. "You!" he roared as Veronica Langtree walked into the basin. Leaping up, he made as if to attack her, but stopped when Trench leveled a rifle at him.

At his outcry, his three daughters rose and spun, Dorette and Ava brandishing their rifles. They trained them on the blonde, who stopped short even as Otis darted in front of her and held a hand aloft.

"No shootin'! Not unless you want every Mohave within earshot knowin' exactly where to find us!"

Ava and Dorette hesitated.

Three gunmen caked with dust brought up the rear, each leading two tired horses. One was Crespin, the young killer in the bowler hat. Another had a wide blood stain on his right shoulder.

"What are you waitin' for?" Luke railed at Dorette and Ava. "Don't fall for their tricks! Shoot them before they gun us down!"

Fargo stepped in before blood was spilled. The blonde's hired killers could easily have shot them before they realized the gunmen were there, yet Langtree hadn't given the word to open fire. She had to have a reason, and Fargo wanted to hear what it was. "No shooting!" he commanded. "Let's find out what they want."

Veronica smiled coldly at the prospector. "It's nice to see that one of you has some brains." Her once immaculate riding outfit was covered with dirt, her hair disheveled, her boots scuffed. A rifle hung from the crook of her left arm, but she made no attempt to bring the gun to bear. "We don't have much time, Luke Gantry, so pay attention. This area is swarming with Mohaves. They outnumber us by a hundred to one. If we're to get out of here alive, we need to join forces—"

Luke snorted. "Hook up with you? After all you've done? Woman, you must take me for an idiot. You just want to get us in your clutches so you can torture us to learn the location of my strike. Well, it won't work. I'm too smart for you."

"As smart as a jackass," Veronica declared. "What good is that gold to any of us if we're not alive to spend it? The Mohaves damn near overran us back there. We barely got out with our lives, and had to head in this direction because every other avenue of escape was cut off. Luckily, Otis found your trail."

"And you followed it all the way here," Luke said. "How kind of you to lead the Mohaves right to us."

Veronica rolled her eyes. "They would have found you anyway. Your tracks stood out as plain as day." She glanced anxiously at the opening. "I figure we have fifteen minutes at the most before they catch up."

Fargo saw Otis lower his rifle. Trench and the rest held back, staring out the gap. There was no doubt in his mind that the blonde was sincere. "What do you have in mind?" he asked.

"A truce, until we're in the clear," Veronica said. "Working together, we might be able to fight our way out. Alone, we'll all be dead in no time."

It made sense to Fargo. The blonde and her gun sharks had as much to gain by an alliance and everything to lose if they didn't work together. The extra guns alone increased the odds of getting out alive. "I like the idea," he admitted.

"Well, I sure as hell don't!" Luke said. "I know her better

than you do, Fargo. The second our backs are turned, we'll be hit over the head and trussed up. Mark my words. Joinin' forces will get us killed. My girls and me ain't about to do any such thing."

Dorette moved closer to Fargo. "Speak for yourself, Pa. You've made it plain that you don't want anything to do with us, that we're on our own from now on. So be it. I'm siding with Skye."

"Me, too," Ava said.

"Fine! Get yourselves killed," Luke fumed. "Just don't expect me to shed any tears over your corpses."

Crespin, who was nearest the opening, suddenly announced, "The Mohaves are coming, Miss Langtree! A whole passel of them. And they're right on our trail."

Veronica hurried to her animal, which Otis held as she climbed on. "Mount up, everybody," she directed. "If we try to make a stand of it here, we'll all be buzzard bait by nightfall."

Fargo draped the water skin over his shoulder before stepping to the horses. Taking the reins to Willa's, he held them out to Dorette and Ava. "The two of you will ride this one," he said.

Willa was quick to object. "What the hell are you doing? That's mine."

"Not anymore." Fargo had no time to argue. The younger sisters had to leave while they still could.

Luke took a step toward him. "Where I come from, any man guilty of horse stealin' has his neck stretched."

"Take it up with the law if you get out of this alive," Fargo said, swinging up.

Langtree and the gunmen were all set to go. She took the lead without being asked. Fargo let Dorette and Ava precede him. Their father stubbornly stood there glaring, but a hint of doubt crept over Willa's features.

"Pa?" she said.

"Let them go. I know what I'm doing."

To the north a war whoop rent the hot air. Fargo cut to the right as lithe forms bounded toward them. The warriors were not quite in bow range, so he held his fire. He preferred to save his ammo for when it was really needed.

The brief rest had done wonders for the Ovaro. The stallion effortlessly maintained the swift pace set by Langtree. The horse ridden by the sisters, however, showed its fatigue early on, and quickly grew worse. Within a couple of miles it began to falter. Fargo stayed alongside them in case it collapsed. When it stumbled for the second time, he called out, "Slow down, Veronica! We'll kill these animals if we don't."

The blonde glanced over a slender shoulder. She did not appear pleased, but she did as he wanted.

On through the grueling, burning afternoon they fled. Twice they stopped briefly to rest. Several times they saw Mohaves, always far off, always to the west or the east.

"I reckon now I know how cattle feel," Otis commented, after a small band of copper-hued warriors was glimpsed paralleling their course.

"How's that, old man?" Crespin asked.

"Those Injuns are herdin' us just like Texans herd longhorns," Otis elaborated. "They're pushin' us deeper and deeper into the desert, into their own country. They're crafty, these devils. They aim to wear us down to where we'll be too weak to put up a fight, so they can capture us without any fuss. Then they'll have their fun."

The young gunman patted his revolver. "Speak for yourself. They're not getting their hands on me if I can help it."

Ava and Dorette kept glancing back, and Fargo knew why. Even after all that had happened, they hoped their father and sister would overtake them. But Luke and Willa never showed. Fargo figured that the prospector's mule-headed pride had finally been the death of him.

Evening found them in the middle of the great desert, surrounded by a sea of baked earth and sand. Volcanic outcroppings dotted the countryside. It was as black and alien a landscape as Fargo had ever come across, worse than the inhospitable deserts of New Mexico, hotter than the arid reaches of Sonora, south of the border. That anyone could live there was amazing enough.

That an entire tribe *thrived* there said a lot about Mohave character.

The setting sun painted the western horizon brilliant bands of pink, orange, and red. Under different circumstances, Fargo would have admired so fine a sunset. This day he hardly noticed. He was on the lookout for a suitable place to make camp.

A rock mass promised to be the best spot. Resembling the great mesas of Arizona and elsewhere, this one was no bigger than a large hill. But three sides were too steep for men on foot to scale. And the fourth, an incline so severe they had to climb down to lead their mounts to the top, was not covered with boulders or other debris. They could spot anyone who tried to sneak up on them.

The horses were bunched in the middle. Veronica posted three of her men around the rim. There was no wood for a fire, so they had to make do without a hot meal and coffee.

Fargo made a circuit of the perimeter. The Mohaves, if they were still out there, were well hidden. Long shadows slunk from nearby ridges and peaks, and it would not be long before darkness claimed the land.

"See anything?"

Veronica Langtree had removed her jacket and unfastened the top of her blouse to combat the heat. The tops of her magnificent breasts were exposed, but she did not seem to care.

"No," Fargo said, puzzled. Not once all afternoon had she made mention of her vow to make him pay for roughing her up on the escarpment. Since she did not impress him as the type to forgive and forget, he was curious to learn what she was up to.

Veronica stood at his elbow and ran a hand through her slick hair. The movement caused her breasts to bulge against her tight top. "I swear, if I make it out of this alive, I'm treating myself to the longest cold bath in human history."

"If you weren't fixing to kill me, I might join you," Fargo said brazenly.

The blonde smiled. As always, the mirth did not light her

eyes. "We have a truce, remember? I'll honor my end until we've given the Mohaves the slip. After that—" She shrugged.

Trench was watching them closely, a hand on his fancy pistol.

"I hope all your men feel the same way," Fargo mentioned. "I'd hate to get a slug in the back when my guard is down."

Veronica shifted and observed the tall gunman. "Don't worry about Dee. I keep him on a short leash. He won't lift a finger against you unless I tell him to."

"And your father?"

"So long as you're not pointing a gun at me or holding a knife to my throat, Otis doesn't care what you do. He's my protector, but he has his limits. He won't kill someone in cold blood."

"It's a shame you don't take after him more than you do," Fargo said. It was a truthful comment, not intended to insult her. Yet it rubbed a raw nerve. She tore into him as if trying to whittle him down to size with her tongue.

"What do you know? You're a *man*. You haven't had to struggle like I have to get ahead." Her voice dripped venom. "You have no idea how hard it is for women. We have to work three times as hard to go half as far." Pausing, she clasped her hands so tightly that her knuckles turned white. "The only way a woman can make her mark in this world is to be more ruthless than those who would put her in her place. So I've learned to be hard, real hard. Most men hold it against me, and I can see you're no different. Pity. I thought you were." She swiveled as if to leave, but she did not go.

"I won't deny anything you've said," Fargo replied. "It just strikes me as a sad state of affairs when a person gets so soured on life that they don't know how to enjoy it anymore."

For a while Veronica was quiet. "You surprise me, Mr. Fargo. I never would have taken you for a philosopher."

"Live long enough and you learn a few things," Fargo said. Leaving her, he joined Dorette and Ava, who sat a dozen feet from the gunmen, their rifles by their sides.

"What did that hussy want?" the redhead asked suspiciously.

"She was passing the time of day," Fargo answered.

"Don't trust her, Skye," Ava said. "We've heard tales about her escapades. They say she uses men, that she invites them into her parlor and treats them to her charms, then gets rid of them when they've served their purpose. Trench isn't the first gent to be struck blind by all that golden hair."

"I'll keep that in mind," Fargo assured them, although he felt they were barking up the wrong tree. Veronica Langtree had flirted with him when they first met, but that was all. The woman would rather slit his throat than anything else.

Later, when stars twinkled on high and coyotes yipped their nightly chorus, Fargo secretly gave a piece of pemmican to each sister. It was wise, he decided, not to let the gunmen know he had a stash of food or they would insist on sharing equally. And truce or no truce, he wasn't willing to share his small supply with men who had been trying to kill him earlier that very day.

Ava finished hers quickly, but Dorette took her sweet time, sucking and savoring down to the last morsel. She had a thumb-sized piece yet to go and was lifting it to her mouth when footsteps heralded the arrival of another.

"What's that you've got there?" Veronica Langtree asked.

Dorette slipped the piece between her lips, then pried at her upper gum with a thumbnail. "Nothing," she said. "I'm just picking between my teeth."

The blonde winked at Fargo. "Perfect ladies, aren't they? When they're not scratching themselves, they're cleaning their teeth in front of everyone else."

"Be careful, lady," Ava warned. "We won't stand for being poked fun at. Just tell us what you want and go back to your own kind."

Veronica squatted near Fargo. Idly resting a hand on his leg, she said, "It isn't fair that my men should have to stand watch all night. The three of you should take turns, as well." She looked at each of them, and when no one objected, she went on. "We've decided to have two people on two-hour shifts. That way everyone gets to take part and no one goes without too much sleep."

Fargo liked the plan, but not for the reasons the blonde might imagine. The plain truth was that he still didn't trust her. For safety's sake, Ava, Dorette, or him had to be awake at one time or another throughout the entire night. "We'll take our turns," he volunteered.

"How obliging of you," Veronica said with a cryptic smile. She told Ava to stand first watch with Trench. Dorette was to share guard duties with Otis. Fargo came next, but the blonde did not mention who he would be paired with. Whistling softly to herself, she strolled off.

"Lord, that woman is a strange one," Dorette said. "I can never tell what she's thinking from one minute to the next."

The sisters made small talk while Fargo reclined on his saddle and let the cool breeze wash over him. Crespin and the wounded cutthroat were patrolling the rim. The wounded man had been favoring his shoulder all afternoon, leading Fargo to suspect it was infected. Unless they eluded the Mohaves the next day, the gunman would be in grave jeopardy.

A little over an hour went by. Suddenly Crespin shouted. A few seconds later, on the opposite side of the mesa, the other gunman did the same. Everyone rushed to see why they were so agitated.

Three small fires had flared to life off in the darkness, one to the north, another to the east, the third to the west. They formed a perfect triangle. Shadows flitted across them as figures passed back and forth.

"It has to be the Mohaves," Trench declared.

"Lettin' us know they're out there," Otis said.

"What are they burning?" Crespin asked. "I didn't see a lick of wood or brush all day."

Veronica Langtree stepped to the edge of the precipice. "Anyone else besides me notice something peculiar?" she asked of one and all.

Fargo was the only one who answered. "There is no fire to the south."

The blonde nodded. "They want us to think it's the safest way for us to go, that they don't have us cut off in that direction, too. When what they're really trying to do is lure us farther into the desert."

"We can't let them get away with it," one of the gunmen said. "Tomorrow we have to fight our way out to the north or the west. It's our only hope."

On that somber note they walked back to the bedding and settled down for the night. Fargo stayed awake until Ava went to stand guard. Allowing himself to drift off at last, he slept much more soundly than he would have liked. Low voices awakened him; Ava was rousing Dorette. He rolled onto his side, rested a cheek on his hands, and was soon asleep again. It seemed as if only a few minutes had gone by when the stealthy pad of feet brought him up and into a crouch in the blink of an eye, the Colt out and cocked.

Dorette Gantry started. "It's only me, Skye! For God's sake, don't shoot."

"Is it my turn already?" Fargo asked.

"Afraid so." Glancing around to insure no one was looking, Dorette scooted in close and kissed him passionately, her tongue entwining with his. She giggled when she broke for air. "There. That's to make sure you keep me in mind until we get some time to ourselves."

Fargo had to smile. There they were, in the middle of the Mojave Desert, surrounded by hostiles, with little food and less water, and uppermost in her mind was making love to him. Picking up the Henry, he walked to the north rim, passing Trench and Otis along the way. The tall gunman snored loudly, out to the world, but the old-timer had just turned in and was still awake. He cracked an eye and nodded at Fargo.

The wind had grown stronger, as it always did late at night. It buffeted Fargo, nearly gusting his hat from his head. Jamming the hat down, he scoured the countryside for a trace of the three fires. There was none. The warriors had long since extinguished them and turned in.

Stretching, Fargo walked westward along the rim, careful not to step too close to the brink. He saw no one else up and about and wondered if he was the only one standing guard. Then he reached the south end of the mesa, and waiting for him on a flat boulder was a buxom figure whose luxurious golden hair glinted in the starlight.

"There you are," Veronica Langtree said softly. "I was beginning to think you would never show up."

"You can't sleep?" Fargo asked, stopping a few feet away. He didn't know what she was up to, but he knew it couldn't possibly be what it appeared to be.

"We're keeping watch together, silly." She patted the boulder. "Come here. Sit beside me. The Mohaves aren't going to attack until daylight, if then. Let's relax and talk a while."

A tiny voice of warning sounded in Fargo's mind. It had to be a ruse, a way of getting him to relax so she could slip a knife into him when he least expected it.

"What's wrong, big man?" Veronica asked. "I've gone out of my way to be friendly, even after you threw me around like a sack of potatoes. The least you can do is be civil." Again she patted the flat boulder. "Come on. I don't bite."

Fargo knew differently. She was as dangerous a woman as he had ever met. Sitting at arm's length, he said, "I'm surprised you would take a turn standing guard. Isn't this what you pay Trench and the others to do?"

Veronica slid a few inches closer. "I'm here because I want to be. You should be flattered instead of acting as if I'm about to gut you." She scrutinized him, and grinned. "That's it, isn't it? You think I'm up to no good, that I mean to go back on my word?"

"The thought did occur to me," Fargo confessed.

The blonde pouted in sham hurt. "Why, what did I ever do to give you so low an opinion of me?" Abruptly brightening, she laughed long and low, as if at a private joke. "You just don't know better than to look a gift horse in the mouth, do you?"

"What are you talking about?"

Veronica leaned back and sighed. Her hair had been brushed, and she had on a clean shirt. The musky scent of perfume hung heavy in the air. "I've always believed in living my life to the fullest. When I want to do something, I do it. When

I see something that should be mine, I take it. I make a lot of people mad at times, but it can't be helped."

Fargo was at a loss to guess where her talk was leading, so he sat quietly, watching her hands for any sudden movement.

"Since I'm so fond of living, it upsets me that tomorrow all of us might die," Veronica continued. "I'm not ready to pass on yet. There's too much I haven't done, too much I haven't seen."

"What does all this have to do with me?"

"Be patient. I'm getting to that." Veronica slid nearer still, moving almost seductively. "If this is to be my last night on earth, I don't want to spend it sleeping. I'd rather do something that fills me with the thrill of being alive. I'd rather spend my last night enjoying myself, not moping."

There was no denying the obvious. Fargo resisted an urge to pinch himself to see if he was truly awake.

The blonde's hand brushed his thigh. "Who else is there? Trench no longer excites me as he once did. Crespin is a kid. And Stimson is about ready to keel over from his infection." Her fingers rubbed in small circles to the top of his leg. "You should be flattered that I picked you. There are men who would kill for the honor."

Fargo was about to tell her that he wasn't one of them. He was about to say that it was the wrong time and place. He was going to let her know he was not all that interested. But before he could say a word, her hand closed on his manhood and her mouth closed on him.

12

The instant the ravishing blonde touched him, Skye Fargo felt his organ pulse and harden. It gave him pause. He made no attempt to push Langtree away as she began languidly stroking him. She knew just what to do to arouse him to a fever pitch, and in moments his blood was pounding to the carnal beat of raw lust. Her tongue, meanwhile, licked and flicked without cease. Despite himself, Fargo met her ardor with equal passion. When he brought up a hand and clamped it on her right breast, she exhaled loudly through her nose and moved flush against him.

It was insane, Fargo reflected. They were no more than fifty feet from her hired killers and her father. They were supposed to be keeping an eye out for hostile Indians. And most bizarre of all, they were enemies. He had to be crazy to be doing what he was doing. Yet he was not about to stop.

Rolling Veronica onto the boulder, Fargo lay beside her and cupped both of her glorious globes. She quivered, bit his lower lip, and raked his back with her long nails. Squeezing harder than he ordinarily would, he elicited a fluttering moan, which she immediately stifled to keep from awakening the sleepers.

Some women enjoyed rough lovemaking and the blonde was one. Wrapping her fingers in his hair, she twisted, hard, while at the same time she rimmed his mouth with her velvet tongue. Her hands clawed at his clothes, yanking his shirt free so she could roam her fingers up over his iron body. Deep in her throat she cooed in delight. He continued to knead her breasts while she thrust against him. She nibbled his ear, his neck, his shoulder. Then, without warning, she bit his jaw so hard that he thought she had drawn blood.

Fargo drew back to look at her. Veronica grinned impishly and snapped at his cheek. She was like a she-wolf in heat, playful and vicious at the same time. Coupling with her was more like a wrestling match than anything else Fargo could think of. He mashed her breasts hard, so hard that most women would have cried out in pain. All she did was bare her white teeth in a savage grin while writhing in ecstasy.

They grappled. They groped. They rubbed one another roughly enough to take off skin. Veronica wielded her nails like miniature rapiers, digging into his back, his ribs, his thighs. The more pain she caused him, the more aroused it made her. When she buried her nails into his buttocks and he grunted from the lancing pangs, she murmured throatily, "Oh, yes, lover! Oh, yes!"

Fargo eased on top of her and knelt between her legs. Grabbing her hair, he wrenched it as she had wrenched his. He meant to teach her a lesson, to show her that she was being too wild. But it had the opposite effect.

Veronica smiled broadly and said huskily, "That's the way, big man! I like it like that!"

Her fingers dipped to his pants and tugged at his gun belt in growing urgency. Fargo helped, setting the Colt to one side as she drew his pants down around his knees. He stiffened when her warm hand closed on his member. A lump formed in his throat. She pumped him, slowly at first, then with increasing speed.

Fargo came close to exploding. Gritting his teeth, he regained control. It took him a minute to undo her shirt and her underthings, but the delay was worth it. Golden melons spilled out, melons capped by swollen nipples as hard as pebbles. Fargo sucked on each. She squirmed beneath him, her legs opening and closing. He massaged her breasts while lathering her nipples, causing her to buck against him in wanton abandon.

Her stomach was as flat as a pancake, as smooth as glass. Fargo ran his tongue down over her belly, swirled it around her navel, and dropped lower. She was so eager that she tried to lift his head and lower it further still. Refusing to be rushed, he undid her pants, pushed them down, and placed both palms on her creamy thighs. She had long, marvelous legs, legs that went on forever, legs so smooth they were like satin. Caressing them was heaven on earth. He indulged himself for many minutes, and all the while she mewed and quivered.

A low noise suddenly froze Fargo with one hand on her leg, another on her breast. Lifting his head, he saw that Trench had sat up.

"What is it?" Veronica whispered.

"Hush," Fargo said, ready to slide off her if the tall gunman got up. Trench was bound to go for his gun the moment he spotted them, and Fargo did not care to be caught with his pants down. He placed a hand on his Colt.

After a few moments Trench shifted position and lay down again.

Veronica was growing impatient. She gripped Fargo's broad shoulders and gave him a little shake. "Come on, lover. What are you waiting for?"

Fargo did not answer. He waited half a minute to satisfy himself that the gunman had gone back to sleep, then he resumed caressing her splendid thighs and breasts. She found his pole. Delicately as a feather, she fondled him. Soon they both were panting. Fargo slid a hand between her legs, brushing the moist lips of her womanhood, causing Veronica to arch her back and hiss like a cat.

As much as Fargo would have liked to take his time, he dared not. The risk of discovery grew with each passing moment. Without any further foreplay, he thrust two fingers into her, jamming them to the knuckles. She loved it. Gripping his arm, she drove herself against his hand. Her red lips parted. The tip of her luscious tongue poked out. She was lost in sexual bliss and hungering for more.

Fargo stoked her inner flames as a person might stoke a furnace, firing her to new heights. Veronica thrashed. She bucked. She clawed his shoulders, neck, and back. Tiny rivulets of blood trickled down his back. When their mouths met, it was like the joining of two panthers. There was no softness, no sense of romance. They tried to overpower one another through sheer sexual prowess. And in this Fargo proved more than a match for her.

Veronica was gasping and softly gurgling when at long last Fargo alighted his manhood. He did not enter her gently. He rammed into her as if trying to cleave her in half, knowing she preferred it that way. Veronica went into a frenzy, tossing her head and heaving against him with so much vigor they nearly toppled from the boulder. He braced his knees to keep from falling, pinned her shoulders to keep her from sliding all over the place, and pounded into her to his heart's content.

The blonde was exquisite. She gave as good as she got, matching his ardor with an elemental desire few women would permit themselves to feel. True to her word, she lived every second to its fullest.

Fargo did not even try to pace himself. He just let himself go, spearing his throbbing organ into her core again and again and again. Their mouths fused. Her tongue glued itself to him. All of that, combined with the friction of her breasts on his chest, inflamed him to a peak he had seldom reached. A keg of black powder was set to explode between his legs, and all he could do was wait for the blast.

Veronica went over the brink first. She threw back her head and opened her mouth as if to scream, but fortunately she had the presence of mind not to. Her body shook violently. Those superb legs of hers looped around Fargo's waist and pressed him close.

Not that Fargo was going anywhere. His own explosion followed shortly after hers. It was more than a keg, it was five kegs, maybe ten. It was the explosion of all explosions. He pumped into her for minutes, longer than he had ever lasted before, draining himself dry. Even after he was spent, he pumped in reflex, pumping until he was too tired to pump anymore. Collapsing on top of her, he sucked in air.

"Not bad," Veronica breathed.

Fargo rolled onto his back and stared up at the stars. The wind chilled him, tingling his skin. He let it. All too soon the sun would rise and he would be so hot he would barely be able to stand it.

Veronica rested a hand on his chest. "No matter what happens, I want you to know that I'm grateful. That was the best ever. If I have to die, I can do so with no regrets."

Draping an arm over his forehead, Fargo made no comment. She was exaggerating, of course, so he did not take her seriously.

"It's too bad we didn't meet under different circumstances," Veronica said quietly. "But that's the way life is. We're always bumping into the right people at the wrong time."

A cough to their rear spurred Fargo into sitting up. None of the sleepers had moved. Even so, to be safe, he swiftly dressed. The blonde did likewise, smoothing her hair when she was done while smirking like a cat that had just downed a favorite morsel.

"I suppose we should stand guard a while, shouldn't we?" she joked.

Fargo strapped on the Colt, then reclaimed the Henry. As he straightened, she grasped his elbow and locked her eyes on his.

"I meant what I just said. But it doesn't change anything. I still intend to find out where Gantry struck it rich. And I'll cut down anyone who stands in my way. Including you."

"I figured as much," Fargo said.

"No hard feelings, I trust?"

"We'll both do what we have to," Fargo responded. She released his arm, winked, and headed to the west, her hips swaying in an enticing fashion.

Fargo walked eastward along the rim. He glanced back at the flat boulder, amazed they had done what they did. He had taken an awful risk. Langtree could just as well have stuck a knife into him as seduced him. He had been playing with fire, and might yet be burned.

Dawn was over an hour off. A mantle of murky darkness still cloaked the country below. Try as he might, Fargo did not see anyone moving. But that did not mean much. The Mohaves were as stealthy as Apaches when they wanted to be. The warriors could close in on the mesa without anyone being the wiser.

Fargo halted on the north side. Here the wind was strongest. Facing into it, he set the stock of the Henry on the ground. It was a rare peaceful moment, the first he had enjoyed in days. Leaning the rifle against his legs, he started to raise him arms to stretch.

Footsteps sounded behind him. Fargo assumed it was Veronica and did not turn right away. Too late, he realized the person was rushing toward him, not walking, and that the tread was heavier than the blonde's would be. A short length of rope swooped down over his head, constricting on his neck, and he was yanked off his feet and pulled backward. The Henry clattered at his feet.

It all happened so fast that Fargo was on his back staring up into the contorted features of Dee Trench before he could collect his wits. The rope gouged in deep, shutting off his breath.

"She's mine, bastard!" the gunman growled. "Nobody lays a hand on her without answering to me!"

Fargo lunged, trying to seize Trench by the head, but the man jerked back. Grabbing Trench's wrists, Fargo strained to break the gunman's hold on the rope. It was no use. Trench had too firm a grip. Fargo's lungs began to ache. His temples pounded.

There had not been time for Fargo to take a breath. In moments he would black out from a lack of air. Still grasping Trench's arms, he suddenly whipped his legs up and over his shoulders. His boots shot past the gunman's head, one to either side, knocking the wide-brimmed black hat off. Trench ducked but maintained his hold.

The very next instant, Fargo twisted his feet so that his spurs pointed at Trench's face. As he swung his legs back, he racked the sharp rowels across both of the gunman's cheeks, digging the points in deep. Blood spurted. Trench snarled and jumped to one side, forced to let go or be raked again. Swiftly Fargo scrambled to his knees and tore the rope from his throat.

Fists flying, Trench waded in. Fargo was rocked by a solid right to the jaw. He blocked a left, dodged a jab, and planted his fist in the gunman's gut. Trench doubled over. A right cross straightened him again. Fargo followed through with a left to the stomach.

The gunman tottered, recovered, and grabbed for his ivory-handled pistols. He stopped dead when a rifle barrel materializied out of nowhere, the muzzle lined up with his nose.

A brittle voice rasped, "Just what in the hell do you think you're doing?"

Fargo had been about to draw. He stopped, the Colt almost out, as Veronica Langtree stepped in close to Trench and poked the tall man with her gun.

"I'm waiting for an answer," the blonde said icily.

Trench blinked and licked his lips. "We had a little disagreement, is all."

"Over what?" Veronica demanded. She tapped her foot, awaiting a reply, but Trench lowered his head, refusing to speak. Veronica glanced at Fargo. "I'm sorry. I saw the whole thing but couldn't get here fast enough to stop him. Why did he jump you?"

"Why do you think?" Fargo rejoined sourly. He remembered Trench sitting up when they were in the middle of their lovemaking. Right then he should have hiked his britches and bowed out, but he had let his passion overrule his common sense. One day, he reflected, his fondness for the opposite sex would be the death of him, if he wasn't careful. Annoyed at himself, he retrieved the Henry.

Veronica had backed off a few steps from Trench, but she did not lower her rifle. "I should blow a hole in you here and now," she declared. "My life is mine to do with as I see fit. You don't own me, Dee. No man does."

"Damn it all—" the gunman began.

"Shut up. I'm not done," Veronica snapped. "Whatever Fargo and I did or didn't do is none of your business. You had no call to attack him. When this is over, if we live and make it back to Los Angeles, I want you to pack your things and leave."

Trench recoiled as if struck. "You can't mean that. Not after all we've meant to each other."

Veronica sneered. "Typical man. You think because I let

you between my legs that you've staked a claim to me for life. It doesn't work that way. I don't love you. I don't even think you're particularly good in bed. All you've ever been to me is someone to do my killing for me."

Fargo almost felt sorry for the man. The truth could be a bitter pill to swallow, and Trench took it hard, withering like a plant under the blazing desert sun. Shoulders slumped, features downcast, the tall man in black pivoted to go, then halted.

"As of this minute it's over between us, lady. I'll admit I'm not the smartest hombre around, so it shouldn't surprise me that you pulled the wool over my eyes. But it does. I thought you really cared. Even after hearing all the stories, I believed you."

Veronica refused to give an inch. "Your mistake. As for our business relationship, it's not over until I say it is. You're still in my employ, and I'll expect you to act accordingly."

"Go to hell."

Fargo watched the humiliated gunman tromp off. "You were awful hard on him," he remarked.

"What do you care? He tried to kill you two minutes ago," Veronica said. She dismissed Trench with a curt wave. "This is nothing new. It happens every time I break off with a man. He'll mope a spell, then get on with his life. They all do, eventually."

"One day one of them might turn on you instead of walking off with his tail tucked between his legs."

The blonde laughed. "It will never happen. None of them is man enough to buck me."

Suddenly Fargo had an urge to rid himself of her company. Bearing westward, he made a circuit of the mesa, not saying a word when he passed her at the southeast corner. Trench had hunkered down near the horses and imitated a statue. Otis was also awake, propped on an elbow, scratching himself. The frontiersman nodded, so Fargo returned the favor. Presently he was back where he had started on the north side. The wind was dying, a prelude to dawn. He peered over the edge and bumped a stone that clattered down the sheer side to the boulders below.

As Fargo took a step back, a shadow detached itself from one of those boulders and darted behind another. In the dim light he could not see the figure all that well, but there was no mistaking the tall, swarthy, near-naked figure for what it was—a Mohave warrior. Kneeling, Fargo removed his hat and lowered his eyes to the edge. It wasn't long before another warrior rushed from spot to spot. Then a third briefly appeared. All of them were making their way westward, toward the slope that linked the top of the mesa to the desert floor.

Fargo ran to the west side. He glimpsed more forms converging from several directions. They vanished as quickly as he saw them, either into gullies or behind boulders. After counting nine he rose and jogged to where Veronica Langtree stood contemplating a pale streak in the eastern sky. "We're in trouble," he announced.

"More than we already were?" the blonde said. "I doubt that's possible."

"The Mohaves are massing at the bottom."

Veronica spun. "Do you think they'll rush us?"

"No. They're too clever for that. They'll wait for us to leave, then spring their trap." Fargo didn't add that the warriors could not have picked a better time to strike. The slope was so steep that riding down it at a gallop invited disaster. They had to walk their mounts to the bottom, giving the Mohaves plenty of time to pick them off.

"Damn. I was hoping they would be content to shadow us for another day or two," Veronica said, hustling toward the sleepers.

Otis had sat up and was honing an old Green River knife. "What's going on?" he inquired.

"Wake the others, then I'll tell you," Veronica said.

Fargo moved to the sisters and roused each one. Ava grumbled and had to be shaken but Dorette bounced to her feet, smiling sheepishly at him.

"I had a dream about you," she whispered. "You wouldn't believe how naughty you were."

Thinking of Langtree, Fargo said, "Yes, I would." He rolled up his bedroll while the two gunmen, Crespin and Stimson, uncoiled stiffly from their blankets, grumbling in protest. Stimson was in a bad way, his face pale and sweaty, his wounded shoulder swollen to twice its normal size.

"I'd give my arm for a cup of coffee," he said.

Crespin took off his bowler to scratch his head. "Why did you wake us so early? We could have slept another half hour by the look of things."

Veronica put her hands on her hips. She glanced toward Trench, who treated her as if she did not exist, then relayed the news Fargo had brought her. Otis, the gunmen, and the Gantrys all commenced talking at once, asking questions or voicing suggestions as to what they should do. She silenced them with an imperious gesture. "One at a time. If anyone has an idea how we can get out of this with our hides intact, I'm willing to listen."

Fargo did not take part in the general confusion. While they chattered like chipmunks, he threw his saddle blanket and saddle on the Ovaro and tied his bedroll in place. No one noticed him until he raised a stirrup to give the cinch another pull.

"What about you, big man?" Veronica Langtree asked. "You haven't said one word, but you must have some notion of what we should do."

Facing them, Fargo was aware that before the day ended most or all of them would not be alive. "The Mohaves aren't fools. They won't risk losing any more men when the sun and the heat can do their job for them. They'll pin us down here until we're so weak from no food and water we can't lift a finger to fight back."

Crespin frowned. "So what you're saying is that we might as well start digging our graves now."

"No. I'm saying that we do the last thing they'll expect," Fargo responded.

"And what might that be, friend?" The question came from Otis.

Fargo had given their predicament a lot of thought and reached the only conclusion possible. "We mount up and head down that slope like bats out of hell. If we time it right, we can take them by surprise." Everyone stared at him as if he had eaten loco weed, so he went on. "It's our only chance. Some of us probably won't make it, but it's better than sitting up here until we're too weak to cock a gun."

The young gunman in the bowler cackled. "Why don't we just sprout wings and fly?" He stabbed a finger at the west rim. "No horse can handle a slope like that."

"The Mohaves are thinking the same thing. It gives us our edge."

"Edge?" Crespin exploded. "It will get us killed, is what it will do. How do you expect us to shoot and work the reins at the same time?"

Dorette cleared her throat. "What about Ava and me, Skye? We have to ride double."

"Your sister's arm is still too sore for her to use well, so she'll go with me," Fargo said.

Crespin, Stimson, and Ava all had something to say, but Veronica Langtree silenced them. Striding to the center of the circle, she declared, "Yes, his idea is crazy. Yes, most of us are going to die. But we have no other choice. So saddle up, people. And let's see if we can send a few of those savages straight to hell before they return the favor."

13

Skye Fargo had a plan, and for it to work they had to wait until after sunrise before making their desperate bid to escape. Once everyone had saddled up, he had them walk their horses to within ten feet of the west rim and ground-hitch the animals until the right moment arrived. Rifles were loaded. Revolvers were checked. Otis wedged the Green River knife under his wide leather belt, just so it "would be handy for pokin; a few heathens."

They were all on edge, some more so than others. Crespin paced like a caged cougar and kept patting his pistol. Veronica regarded everyone with her typical icy, detached air. Trench did not say a word to a soul. His face shielded by his hat brim, he stood off by himself with his arms folded.

Ava insisted on giving some of the precious water to Stimson, and Fargo did not object. The gunman was so weak that he could barely stand. His shoulder and arm were swollen worse than ever, the wound black and putrid.

A few minutes before sunrise, as Fargo was shoving the Henry into his saddle scabbard, Dorette came over.

"I want the truth. Why are you letting my sister ride with you?"

"I told you," Fargo said.

The redhead arched an eyebrow. "You were blowing smoke. Her arm is better than it's been in days. She could ride with me if she had to." Dorette stepped closer. "You're doing this so we'll have a better chance of getting out of this alive, aren't you? The two of us aren't as good riders as you are. You're putting your own life at risk on our account."

Fargo was spared from having to admit the truth by the timely approach of Crespin.

"The sun is starting to come up. Shouldn't we mount and get ready?"

"We have to wait until it clears the horizon," Fargo detailed. "It'll be another fifteen to twenty minutes yet." He made certain the rifle was secure and was about to turn when he noticed his bedroll. It sparked a memory from the time he visited the Gila River country, and an idea occurred to him.

Crespin had not left. Nervously scanning the sky, he said, "Are you sure you know what you're doing? Why not go now, while it's still dark. Once the sun is up, those Injuns will be able to drop us like flies."

"We need to be able to see to make it down the slope in one piece," Fargo explained. "And if we time it right, the sun will work in our favor."

"How so?"

"Wait and see," was all Fargo would say. Moving to the rim, he dropped onto his belly and snaked forward until the boulders below were revealed. Not so much as a mote of dust stirred, but he wasn't fooled. Dozens of Mohaves were down there, their eyes fixed on the top of the mesa. Just as he had counted on.

Returning to the horses, Fargo removed his bedroll, rolled out the blankets, and began folding them into large squares. Some of the others, curious, came over to watch.

Otis squatted. "What are you doing there, young fella? Fixin' to go back to bed?"

Fargo chuckled. "It's a trick I learned from the Mexicans who live in Apache country. When they know Apaches are around, they take their serapes or old blankets, fold them a few times, and tie them to their chests and backs."

The old frontiersman grinned. "I get it. That way, if an Apache arrow hits them, it gets slowed by all that paddin' and doesn't go in deep."

"Does it work?" Crespin asked doubtfully.

"Not all the time," Fargo admitted. "But every little bit helps." He finished and beckoned to the Gantrys. Cutting lengths of rope, he tied one triple-folded blanket to Ava's back, another to Dorette's back, and a third to the redhead's chest.

"What about you?" she asked.

"I'm out of blankets," Fargo said. With Ava riding behind him, his back would be protected. As for the front of him, whether or not he took an arrow was in the hands of fate.

Otis, Crespin, and Stimson chose to do as Fargo had suggested. Veronica refused until her father nagged her into attaching a blanket to her back. Trench did not seem to care enough to fit himself with extra protection.

By then the blazing sun had risen. Fargo noted the angle between the horizon and the mesa, and ordered everyone to climb on their animals. Stimson had to be given a boost by Crespin and Otis. The stricken gunman was so sick that he swayed, barely able to stay on.

"I'll never make it like this. Someone tie me to my saddle so I'll have a fighting chance."

Otis did as the man wanted.

The horses were far enough back from the edge that the Mohaves could not see them. Fargo held the Ovaro's reins firmly and glanced over a shoulder at the eastern sky. Timing was critical. They could not go until the sun rose high enough. It had to clear the mesa rim, so the warriors below would be temporarily blinded by the brilliant glare when they looked up.

The others sat their mounts grimly, all with weapons in hand, except Trench, who made no effort to draw either of his expensive pistols. He was at the south end of the line, near Veronica and Otis. Next came the two gunmen, then Fargo and Dorette. Some of the horses pranced nervously, as if they sensed what was about to occur.

No one uttered a word. The air grew hotter by the minute. Fargo shifted a little forward to accommodate Ava, who leaned against his back. Dorette mustered a feeble smile, then touched the bandanna covering the base of her throat, and her scar. Somewhere an insect buzzed, the first they had encountered since entering the Mojave Desert.

Then came the moment Fargo had been waiting for. The sun

hung poised in the sky at the proper angle. Lifting the reins, he raked the stallion with his spurs, jabbing them much harder than he ordinarily would, so hard that the pinto broke into a gallop from a standing start and flew over the edge without any hesitation.

The rest were only a few yards behind.

Fargo concentrated on the steep slope unfolding under him. He had to lean back so the Ovaro would not lose its balance. Ava molded her body to his, doing as he did. She was smart enough to realize that a single mistake on her part doomed them both. The stallion slid toward the desert floor at a dizzying rate, dirt and dust spraying in its wake.

The moment they appeared, a war whoop rent the air. Mohaves materialized, seemingly out of thin air, some armed only with clubs and lances, but far too many with stout bows. The first arrows rained down before Fargo and the others had descended ten feet.

A rifle blasted. Someone cursed lustily. Fargo was hard-pressed to stay on the hurricane deck of his mount. The treacherous footing made the stallion slip and stumble, and Fargo came close to being pitched over its head. Almost in his ear, Ava's rifle went off. He glimpsed a Mohave go down, but it was small comfort. There had to be thirty or forty ringing the bottom.

More guns added to the din. Crespin was hollering like a madman. Otis yipped, Comanche fashion. The hail of arrows thickened. A horse whinnied stridently and there was a resounding crash. Fargo risked a glance and saw Stimson's animal down, three shafts jutting from its chest.

Stimson had been pinned and was frantically trying to free his leg. Before he could, two arrows struck the blanket tied to his back. The gunman jerked to the impact but the padding spared him. Momentarily. As he pushed against his animal's neck, another arrow caught him low under the left eye, the tip bursting out the rear of his cranium.

Fargo had to grip the reins with both hands to guide the pinto. It swerved to the right, nearly colliding with Dorette's horse. She had an arrow sticking from the blanket tied to her chest, but she did not appear to be severely hurt. Her rifle blasted in regular cadence.

A scream drew Fargo's attention to the south. It was so shrill, so high-pitched, that he mistakenly assumed Veronica Langtree had taken a shaft. But it wasn't the blonde. It was Crespin.

An arrow transfixed the young gunman's left arm above the elbow. In anguish, he flapped it and screeched while firing wildly at the warriors. None of his shots scored. And in his frenzied state, he forgot to keep a tight rein on his animal. The horse tripped, squalled, and went down, tumbling Crespin head over heels. He slid to a stop amid a cloud of dust. Dazed, Crespin rose unsteadily, swung toward the Mohaves, and was met by a valley of arrows that no amount of extra padding could withstand. Bristling shafts as a porcupine does quills, he oozed to the ground and was still.

All this Fargo took in out of the corner of an eye. He had his hands too full with simply staying alive to help the others. A narrow fissure loomed in his path and he hauled on the reins, cutting the pinto to the left to miss it. At the same moment, a burly Mohave ran toward him with a lance cocked to throw. Fargo could not let go of the reins to shoot, and Ava was looking in another direction.

The warrior thought he had them. The man grinned as he started to whip his arm in an arc. But a pair of booming reports killed the grin, even as the pair of holes that blossomed in his chest killed him. Soundlessly, the Mohave crumpled.

Dorette had done the shooting. Veering to the north, she worked the trigger guard of her Spencer, which served the same purpose as the lever on Fargo's Henry. Without missing a beat, she fired again.

Fargo was nearing the bottom. Arrows cleaved the air on all sides, as thick and fast as a swarm of hornets. Two Mohaves reared in front of him, both with arrows notched to sinew bowstrings. In reflex, he stroked the Colt twice, coring the brain of each.

Bedlam reigned. Guns thundered all along the slope. The wavering neighs of frightened horses, the fierce whoops of the warriors, and shouts and oaths born of blood lust added to the din. Clouds of gunsmoke and dust choked the air. It was chaos. There was no other word for it. And through it all Fargo somehow stayed in the saddle and reached the desert floor unscathed.

Ava was firing her rifle as fast as she could. Suddenly, it went empty and she ducked low to reload.

Off to the south a man cried out. Otis had been pierced by a shaft high on the right thigh. The tip had gone through his leg, embedding itself in his saddle. He was pinned fast, unable to dismount even if he'd wanted to. Going on, Otis was almost to the bottom when a half-dozen warriors sprang toward him. One he killed with a slug to the sternum. Another he winged. The third time, the hammer fell on an empty chamber. Since reloading was impossible, he drew the Green River knife to meet a trio of flying forms with his slashing blade. The Mohaves ripped him from his horse and Otis went down fighting.

Fargo wanted to go to the frontiersman's aid, but he had his hands full with four warriors sweeping toward him from different directions. In addition, between the Ovaro and Otis were over a dozen more. It would be suicide to try to reach the oldtimer.

Someone else was closer. Shrieking like a lynx, Veronica Langtree charged the knot of Mohaves on top of her father. She felled two of them, which enabled Otis to struggle to his knees. Out of the throng sprinted a warrior holding a hefty club. Veronica yelled a warning, but it was too late. The club crushed the frontiersman's skull as if it were made of paper.

For a few seconds, Veronica was too stunned to move. The Mohaves surged toward her, the nearest reaching for her mount's bridle. The man's fingers were inches away when a new element intruded.

An ivory-handled Colt in either hand, Trench barreled into the warriors, blazing away, firing right and left at anything that moved. He mowed down four of them in as many seconds, then leaned over and smacked the blonde's horse on the rump. The horse fled northward, knocking several Mohaves aside. He followed, covering her.

Fargo had his own hands full. He burst through the ring of four warriors by putting a bullet into one and ramming the Ovaro into another. Instantly he wheeled the pinto to the north, where the Mohaves were fewest. Dorette had already fled in that direction, opening a path for him. He saw her race into the clear and look back. Ava, having reloaded, was firing rapidly.

A bronzed warrior armed with a knife suddenly appeared on top of a ten-foot-high boulder. Howling like a maddened wolf, the man flung himself at Fargo, his arms outstretched, the blade gleaming in the bright sunlight.

Fargo twisted and fanned the Colt with his left palm. The Mohave was so close that the slug blew a sizable chunk out of the top of the man's head and flipped him backward into the boulder. The warrior's body had not yet smacked on the ground when a second Mohave darted into the open, holding a lance in both hands, level at his waist. His intent was to spear the weapon into the stallion's side, but Fargo thwarted him with a shot to the right cheek that spun the man around and dropped him where he stood. Yet another Mohave leaped forward, a war club upraised. Fargo and Ava fired at the same time, and an invisible hand picked up the warrior and flung him into the dirt.

Then the stallion was also in the clear, which was just as well for Fargo since he had expended the cartridges in his pistol. He reloaded while galloping pell-mell across the desert, close behind Dorette. A look back confirmed that Veronica and Trench had also survived and were in swift flight.

Cries of outrage erupted from the Mohaves when they saw their quarry escaping. Many chased after Fargo and the others on foot. For a short distance the fleet warriors managed to keep the horses in sight, but presently the greater stamina of the animals prevailed and the Mohaves were left breathing their dust.

Fargo felt sorry about the old man. Out of Veronica's bunch, Otis had been the only one he genuinely liked. Replacing the last spent cartridge, he slid the Colt into his holster and knuckled down to the task of putting a lot of distance between the Mohaves and them. His main worry was that more warriors might be up ahead.

Across the burned landscape they sped, Dorette slowing so Fargo could catch up. They shied away from outcroppings, where Mohaves could be concealed. Galloping along in open country, they soon covered more than two miles. Pursuit had long since ended. In front of them the wasteland stretched to the Panamint Mountains, far in the distance.

To conserve their mounts, Fargo slowed to a walk. Both horses were perspiring heavily, exhausted. He patted the Ovaro, then faced the redhead. "Are you hurt?"

Dorette's brow knit. She looked down, laughed at the sight of the arrow sticking from the blanket, and said, "Would you believe that in all the excitement I forgot about this thing?" A sharp twist was all it took for her to tear the shaft loose. "No blood," she said, showing him the tapered point. "I reckon I'll live."

Ava sagged against Fargo. "Lordy, I hope I never go through another ordeal like that again. I thought for sure we were goners."

To the northwest stood a solitary stone monolith over twenty feet high and half that in diameter. It offered shade from the relentless sun and the added benefit that no one could get near it without being seen. Fargo angled in its direction, saying, "The horses need to rest before we push on."

"I can't wait to reach San Francisco," Dorette said. "It will seem like heaven after what we've been through." She beamed like a little girl who could not wait to receive a holiday gift. "I'm no longer upset about having to leave the gold behind. Being rich doesn't matter all that much anymore. Being alive does."

"Just don't put the cart before the horse," Ava advised. "We're not safe yet."

Fargo concurred. Many miles of desert lay before them, as well as days of hard travel through the mountains to the coast. He reined up at the base of the monolith, eased Ava down, then slid off himself. The acrid odor of gunsmoke lingered in his nostrils and he inhaled deeply to clear them. Untying the water skin, he handed it to the redhead. "You first. Three sips is all you get."

Ava sank down with her back to the massive stone slab. "I wish that Crespin fella had lived," she said ruefully. "I thought he was kind of cute."

Dorette froze in the act of raising the water skin to her mouth. "Are you forgetting that he tried to shoot you?"

"So? Just because someone tries to kill you doesn't mean the two of you can't be friendly."

Fargo would have laughed if not for his interlude with Veronica Langtree. The blonde and Trench were sixty yards out, moving at a turtle's pace, arguing. He imagined they were squabbling over their breakup and did not give them another thought. When it came his turn to drink, he only took one sip, capped the skin, and hung it on his saddle. The sisters sat next to one another, talking quietly and giggling, giddy from their narrow escape. He knew the feeling well, having been through more harrowing incidents than he cared to dwell on.

Veronica Langtree and Trench reined up a dozen feet out. Both were worn out and caked with dust. Veronica smiled, then said, "We did it, didn't we?"

Fargo nodded, draping his arms on his saddle. He scanned the desert for their enemies, but saw no one.

"So now we're back where we began," Veronica resumed. "Which means I can pick up where I left off." She had been holding her rifle across her thighs. Now she streaked it to her shoulder, and as she did, the gunman palmed his fancy hardware with a speed few men could rival.

Dorette and Ava made grabs for their rifles, stopping when Veronica fired a warning shot into the dirt at their feet.

"Don't even think it, ladies. I only need one of you to find the site. Cooperate, though, and both of you will live. You have my word."

Fargo was upset with himself for being so careless. He should have anticipated her treachery. Veronica had told him that once they were out of danger, the truce was off. Why hadn't he remembered the fact sooner? He yearned to go for his gun, but was dissuaded by the steady barrels of Trench's twin nickel-plated revolvers.

Ava started to rise. "You can go to hell! Shoot one of us if you want. Shoot both of us, you back-stabbing vixen. But we won't lead you to our pa's diggings."

"Never!" Dorette added.

"Is that so?" Veronica studied the pair awhile. Glancing at Trench, she said, "Did you hear, Dee? They have more backbone than I counted on. I do believe they would let me kill them before they would reveal the location."

Trench offered no reply.

Bending low, Veronica uttered a low, wicked laugh. "Your ploy would work, ladies, if I didn't know what I do. Namely, that the two of you have grown rather fond of our mutual friend." Her rifle swiveled toward Fargo's chest. "I've seen how you act, how you fawn over him all the time. So I'm willing to bet his life that you'll agree to do as I want if I agree to let him live." The hammer clicked.

Dorette leaped to her feet, about to hurl herself at Langtree, but Ava seized her legs and held on. "You leave Skye out of this!" she said. "This is between you and us."

"Sorry, dearie," Veronica taunted. "As your sweet Skye will confirm, when I want something, I don't stop until I get it. And I want to know where your father struck gold. So either agree to lead me there, or you can watch me fill him with lead, starting at the knees and working my way up." She aimed at Fargo's left kneecap to emphasize her point.

Fargo did not move. He looked at Trench, who would not meet his gaze, then at the sisters, who were horrified. Ava had let go of Dorette, and the redhead was gnawing on her lower lip while clenching and unclenching her hands.

"I'm waiting," Langtree said.

Ava pounded the ground. "I hate you!"

"That's not what I want to hear," Veronica said. "But if that's your answer, so be it." Steadying her rifle, she lightly touched her finger to the trigger.

Dorette took a step and threw her arms up. "Wait! All right!

We'll do as you want! We'll take you there, provided you won't hurt him."

Aglow with the flush of triumph, Veronica slowly lowered her rifle. "Your kind are so predictable. I'd let Fargo die rather than allow anyone to get their hands on all that gold."

"What are your plans for me?" Fargo asked. "What now?"

"Why, you're coming with us, lover. You're my insurance that these two will do as I want them to do. Once they have, you can ride off to wherever your little heart desires."

It was a lie. Fargo doubted that he would be alive two minutes after Langtree set eyes on the pit. The same went for the sisters. Yet they had to play along in the hope that Veronica and the gunman would make a mistake they could turn to their advantage. He elevated his hands on being told to do so, then had to submit to being disarmed by Trench.

"Mount up," Veronica commanded.

Once again Fargo found himself a captive. Once again he was forced to ride off across the desert in a direction he did not want to go. Once again, whether he lived or died depended on the whims of a cruel killer. All his effort, all the hardship he had endured, had been for nothing. He was right back where he had started—unarmed, held at gunpoint, and facing the specter of impending death.

14

Skye Fargo did have one thing to be thankful for. This time he did not have to put up with having his wrists tied. Trench wanted to, but Veronica told the gunman not to bother, that if the Mohaves appeared, Fargo would need his hands free to do some hard riding.

For the rest of that day they bore northward, toward Death Valley. Veronica was so eager to reach the vein that she insisted they keep going even after the sun set. Thanks to the pale glow of a quarter-moon, they were able to see well enough to avoid any mishaps.

About nine that night the blonde called a halt. A cold camp was made in a gully, and Fargo, Dorette, and Ava had their ankles bound. Langtree and Trench took turns standing guard. At the crack of dawn everyone was back in the saddle. The rest had done them little good. They were all still tired, as well as hungry and thirsty. Langtree didn't care. She spurred them on, her greed overriding all other impulses.

Toward the middle of the afternoon two events took place that forced a delay. The first was when they came on a pair of rattlers basking in the sun. The snakes were longer than Fargo's arms and thicker than his wrists, and zipped toward nearby rocks with incredible speed. But as quick as they were, Trench was quicker. Twin blasts from his pistols stopped them both. From a boot he drew a butcher knife with which he chopped off their heads and tails and skinned them. The chunks of meat were wrapped in the skin to keep until later.

Soon after resuming their trek, the second incident took place. Veronica led them into a jumbled outcropping. There, the Ovaro suddenly lifted its head. Fargo likewise perked up, the dank scent he detected telling him that there was water close at hand. "Hold up," he declared, drawing rein.

Veronica halted and glanced sharply at him. "Why? What are you trying to pull?"

"Don't you smell it?" Fargo asked. Twisting this way and that, he pinpointed the possible source and moved toward a space between a high rock wall and a boulder.

"I'm warning you," Veronica said. "If you're up to something, just remember that Trench is right behind you."

How could Fargo forget? The gunman watched him like a red hawk would prey it was going to swoop down on. He could practically feel Trench's eyes boring into his back every minute of the day.

Skirting the boulder, Fargo discovered a small tank nestled next to it. He was off the pinto in a flash and kneeling to dip a hand in the water. It was warm and flat and had a faint mineral taste, but it was fit to drink.

At Fargo's yell the others came on the fly. Veronica let out a squeal of joy as her parched mount made a beeline for the pool. Leaping, Fargo grabbed the bridle in time. "We should fill the water skin and quench our own thirst before we let the animals drink," he proposed. By rights, their horses should go first, but there was plenty for all, and the animals were bound to dirty the tank.

For a brief while they acted like children, splashing and dipping their heads under the surface and laughing at their own antics. Except for Trench, who stood to one side with his brawny hands resting on the smooth butts of his pistols. He did have a comment to make, which was, "We might as well stay the night here, Veronica. Who knows how long it will be before we find water again."

Langtree grumbled but bowed to common sense. She ordered Dorette to cook the snake meat. A patch of dry grass and weeds made for a fine fire, and before long the tantalizing aroma of roasting meat had Fargo's mouth watering and his stomach growling. All of them stared at the makeshift spit like a pack of starved wolves at prime prey.

As famished as Fargo was, the portion he was given did not fill him up. It was enough, though, to appease his hunger and give him a pleasant feeling of lethargy. After eating, he lay on his back with his hands on his stomach, trying to remember if he had ever eaten rattlesnake so delicious.

Fargo's high spirits evaporated when Trench tied him for the night. It brought home the fact that instead of going meekly to the slaughter, he should be racking his brain for a way of turning the tables on his captors. So far he had done exactly as they wanted, to lull them into thinking he was not going to be a problem. It was high time he did something.

But no chance presented itself the next morning when they headed out shortly after sunrise. Nor did Trench let down his guard during the forenoon hours, as they plodded across the burning earth in single file.

They had started the day refreshed. By noon they were dying for a drink, and the horses hung their heads in fatigue. In the shade of a knoll they rested. No sooner did they take a seat than Veronica stalked up to the sisters and demanded, "How much longer until we reach your father's find?"

Ava shrugged. "If we push hard, we can be there by tomorrow afternoon."

"That soon?" Veronica said, her eyes sparkling. Slapping the stock of her rifle, she snapped, "On your feet, then, all of you! We're not wasting another minute."

The afternoon temperature hovered near one hundred and ten. That did not stop Langtree from driving them relentlessly onward. Fargo, near the end of the line, pulled his hat brim low and breathed shallowly. Trench had the water skin, or he would have treated himself to a drink. Glancing back, he saw the gunman staring at him, as always. "Keep it up and I'm liable to think you don't trust me," he cracked.

"I don't," Trench said somberly. "We both know that you're just waiting for me to do something stupid."

Fargo could not resist. He nodded at Veronica Langtree and said, "You already have. Hooking up with her again."

"Don't stick your nose where it doesn't belong."

Fargo paid him no heed. "Why, Trench? She came right out and told you that she had no use for you anymore." For a minute the tall gunman was silent, and Fargo thought he would never learn the answer. Then Trench sighed.

"She told me she was sorry. She asked me to forgive her, to work with her again, to split the gold fifty-fifty."

"And you believed her?" Fargo said. He had a secret motive for prying. If he could rekindle the doubt Trench harbored, if he could turn Trench against Langtree, it would work in his favor. "Didn't it dawn on you that the only reason she came crawling back was because she had no one else to rely on? The rest of her men are all dead. Without you, she'd be on her own."

Trench was a long time replying. "I thought of that. It's not important. All that matters is being with her again. She's like no woman I've ever known, Fargo. And I'll stick with her for as long as she'll have me."

"Will you carry out her orders when she tells you to kill us?"

For all his faults, the gunman was as honest as the day was long. "Yes," he stated. "And I won't lose a wink of sleep, either. So you can forget getting at her through me."

That settled that. Fargo faced front to find Veronica smirking at him. Beyond her, circling low in the sky, were several buzzards. He pointed them out.

"So?" Langtree said. "They're probably feeding on a dead animal."

She was wrong. It turned out that over a dozen of the ungainly, ugly scavengers were already on the ground, clustered in twos and threes, yards apart. One of those clusters was directly in their path. The vultures hissed at the approaching horses, then took to the air with a ponderous flapping of their large wings. The object they had been feasting on came into view.

"What the hell!" Veronica Langtree blurted.

It was a human arm, or what was left of one. The sharp beaks of the large birds had ripped the flesh to shreds and cleaned several of the fingers down to the bone. Enough skin remained to identify the victim as white.

The blonde prodded her horse toward another cluster of buzzards. They stood their ground until she was almost on top of them, then soared into the air. This time the vultures had been gorging themselves on a severed leg. Buckskin pants lay in tatters around it. Holes had been torn in the boot, but not enough to bare the foot.

"Oh, God!" Ava said, horrified.

Veronica led them to the largest group of buzzards. As they waddled off to take wing, they revealed the grisly remains of a human torso. The shirt had been ripped to bits, the chest eaten down to the sternum. The abdomen was a gaping cavity, the intestines pulled out and left dangling over the chest.

Past the torso was an even ghastlier find. Fargo swallowed bile that tried to rise in his throat.

The eyes had been pecked out, the nose eaten, and the once rosy lips sheared from the mouth, but there was no mistaking the now filthy shock of long hair or the outline of the untouched chin. Of the many ways to die, Willa Gantry had met her end in one of the most terrible. The Mohaves had hacked off her limbs, decapitated her, and left the parts for the scavengers to feed on.

Tears poured from Dorette. "No! Oh, no!" She jumped from her horse and dashed to the head. Impulsively, she reached for it, but caught herself. "Willa!" she wailed, falling to her knees.

"Get back on your horse!" Veronica directed in vain.

Ava slid to the ground and joined her sister. She immediately began scooping at the earth with her hands.

"What do you think you're doing?" Veronica said.

"We're not taking another step until our sister is buried," Ava said. "Shoot us if you like. It won't make a difference. Doing the decent thing by Willa is more important."

Fargo climbed down to help. The stench was sickening. He had to hike his bandanna up over his mouth and nose so he could breathe. The soil was so hard packed that it took the better part of half an hour to make a shallow grave large enough for the head and torso. The legs and arms were placed in a separate hole. Langtree fumed the whole time, but she wisely did not try to force the sisters to go on until they were ready.

"I wonder," Dorette said sadly as she mounted, "if the same thing happened to Pa? Maybe the savages got them both."

From then on they were on the lookout for buzzards or bodies, but saw neither. Veronica made a late camp to make up for the delay. Well before first light she woke them up, let them drink a handful of water, and forged northward.

The day was the hottest yet. If Fargo had to guess, he would have said it was one hundred and fifteen in the few spots of shade. They entered Death Valley within an hour of starting out. As the sun climbed, the hellish, suffocating inferno became almost unbearable. Their horses grew weak and sluggish.

"Keep this up," Fargo said at one point, "and we'll be lucky to reach the site alive."

"Let me worry about that," Veronica rasped.

"How about a drink?" Dorette asked.

"When I'm good and ready," was the blonde's reply.

A dozen times before noon Veronica asked the sisters how much farther they had to go. She was so impatient that she could not sit still. Constantly fidgeting in the saddle, she fingered her rifle, her saddle horn, the animal's mane.

The signs were there for anyone to see, the signs of someone teetering on the brink. Fargo noticed, and he was certain the Gantrys did. Trench, however, carried on as if nothing out of the ordinary were taking place, as if the coldhearted beauty he cared so much about were not being devoured alive by the vilest of human monsters, raw greed.

The afternoon came and went. Veronica grew more and more anxious and cast angry glances at Ava.

Fargo had memorized the landmarks near the gorge. It was a habit, long ingrained, as crucial to his survival in the wilderness as his ability to track game and locate water. So he knew when they were close, and said, "It won't be long now."

"Really?" Veronica said, her features shining with excitement. Her gaze hardened. "It had better be, or I might take it into my head that the three of you have been playing me for a jackass."

As if on cue, the mouth of the gorge materialized off to the right. Ava pointed, saying, "I hope you're happy, witch. Back in there is Pa's vein."

"It's not his anymore," Veronica observed. Rising in the stirrups, she surveyed the mouth and both rims. "Exactly how far back do we have to go?"

Dorette responded. "All the way. We dug a pit at the bottom of a cliff. There's enough gold to make you the richest woman in the country."

A gleeful laugh ripped from Veronica's throat. "Suits me just fine! Soon it will all be mine."

Fargo noticed Trench glance up. For the first time, the gunman's expression was troubled.

"Ours, you mean, don't you?" Trench said.

Veronica nodded, much too hastily. "Of course, Dee. Ours. We agreed to share and share alike, and I aim to abide by our decision."

Anyone could have seen that Langtree had no intention of keeping her word, but there were none so blind as a man in love. Fargo removed his bandanna to wipe his face and neck, then replaced it. The sun sizzled like a frying pan in the western sky, balanced on the horizon. As they wound into the gorge, shadows preceded them. It was as quiet as a tomb. No lizards scuttled about, no snakes were seen. A premonition gnawed at Fargo's mind, and he eyed the bedroll on Trench's horse. In it were all their guns. Somehow, he had to get to that bedroll, and soon.

Presently they came to the final bend. Ava announced as much, and Veronica abruptly drew rein and fixed her rifle on the sisters. "It just dawned on me that I could be blundering into a trap. Your father might be in there, waiting to pick off anyone who comes around the corner. So the two of you will go first. And don't try to call out to him. Now that we're here, both of you are expendable."

But not for much longer, Fargo realized. Once Langtree confirmed the gold was there, she would lose no time in slaying them, or having Trench do it. Intentionally, he slowed, hanging back so the gunman would draw nearer. Pretending there was something wrong with the Ovaro, he stared at its front hooves and said, "What's the matter with you, boy? Why are you starting to limp?"

Dorette and Ava had passed Veronica. Her rifle leveled at their backs, Dorette walked their mount into the final stretch leading to the cliff. No shots rang out. No shouts were heard. No one called their names. Here the shadows were longer and darker. Here the air hung as heavy as the cloak of darkness that would soon descend.

Fargo slowed even more. Trench was doing what the others were doing, peering at the cliff to see the pit. Unwittingly, the gunman came closer. Soon he would be within reach. Fargo bent down as if examining the pinto's legs, and tensed to spring.

"So where is this hole you claimed was here?" Veronica asked, halting. "I don't see it."

Fargo risked a look. They were close enough to the wall for the gaping hole to be obvious, yet it wasn't there. In its place was a mound of fresh earth as wide as the pit had been. Someone had filled the diggings in, filled them in and added dirt to spare. It had taken the Gantrys many months to excavate the huge hole, yet someone had erased every trace of their hard toil in the span of days. Fargo was so startled that he let Trench go by.

"It should be right there," Ava declared, pointing. Astonished, she slid from her horse and stepped cautiously toward the spot. Her sister stayed mounted.

Veronica Langtree also dismounted. "If this is a trick . . ."

"You can see for yourself," Ava said. "Look at all this dirt. Someone has filled it in on us." She stopped cold, gasped, and shrieked a cry ripped from the depths of her soul. *"Pa!"*

Fargo had to see. He spurred the Ovaro past a low boulder. On top of the mound was an oval object caked with dirt and dark stains. In a few more yards he saw it clearly, and halted.

Luke Gantry had been buried alive in the dirt used to fill his previous pit. Only his head stuck out. His hair was matted with dried blood, his face smeared with more. His eyes were gone. Streaming in and out of the sockets, and in and out of his nose, ears, and mouth, were countless ants. Those going in had nothing in their mandibles. Those coming out carried tiny bits of Luke Gantry.

Veronica Langtree walked right up to the mound. "The Mohaves did this. But if they think they can stop me, they have another think coming. It won't take Trench long to dig down to the gold." She threw back her head and cackled, the laugh choking off in a shocked grunt. "*It's them!*" she screamed.

Fargo looked up. Lining the rim above the cliff were over thirty tall, tattooed figures. Fully half of them had arrows notched to their bows. Foremost among them, at the very center, stood the archer who had strayed into the gorge the other day with two fellows and seen them slain by Luke and Willa Gantry.

For a few heartbeats the tableau was frozen. Then Veronica Langtree roared, "I won't let you savages stop me! This gold is mine!" Crouching, she opened fire, working her Spencer feverishly.

All hell broke loose. Piecing war whoops echoed off the walls as shafts rained down, buzzing like bees. The deep shadows at the bottom of the gorge made Fargo and his companions hard for the Mohaves to pick out, or they would have been massacred in the first few seconds. Ava whirled and ran.

Trench, farthest from the pit, could have fled and saved himself. Instead, he vaulted from his horse and raced to help Veronica, his twin pistols blazing.

Fargo was under no obligation to either of them. Cutting the stallion to the left, he swiftly untied one end of the gunman's bedroll and flashed a hand inside. In moments he had his hardware and the rifles belonging to the sisters. Hooves clattered, and Dorette appeared at his side. He shoved her rifle into her hands and was turning to go get Ava when she pounded up astride Veronica Langtree's horse. Without another word, bent low, they sped down the gorge.

Spinning shafts fell like hail. One dug a bloody furrow in Dorette's horse. Another nicked Fargo's hat. There were so many that Fargo did not think they would make it. At any moment he expected to feel searing pain or hear one of the sisters scream. Neither happened. They came to the first bend unharmed, and as they swept around it, Fargo shot a glance back.

Veronica Langtree was on her knees, bent over. Arrows bristled from her neck, her back, her legs. Trench had one arm around her waist and was backpedaling toward his horse, firing as he retreated. Already four or five shafts were embedded in his husky frame. As Fargo looked on, a quartet of Mohave archers took deliberate aim and let their arrows fly at the same instant. Just as the bend cut off Fargo's view, the tall gunman toppled.

Fargo shook himself, as if he were awakening from a bad dream. He galloped on down the gorge, scouring the rim. But no more warriors appeared. Then he reached the entrance, and before them stretched the dry expanse of Death Valley. Into the fading sunlight Fargo galloped, alive and free and happy to be both. By midnight they would reach the Panamint Mountains. In about ten days, San Francisco.

Skye Fargo glanced at the lovely women on either side of him, and smiled. Maybe he would take a little longer. After all he had been through, it was only fair to treat himself.

LOOKING FORWARD!
The following is the opening section from the next novel in the exciting *Trailsman* series from Signet:

THE TRAILSMAN #175
BETRAYAL AT EL DIABLO

El Diablo, Mexico, in 1860—
a vast labyrinth of canyons and blistering heat,
bandidos, thirst, and stalking death,
where legends said the killing land
could burn a man's body and soul to ash . . .

The hawk was floating in a wide circle high in the white-hot sky, a half mile off the trail to the west. There was only one thing that made a hawk spin in the sky like that. Something dead below. Hidden in a mesquite-choked gully. And it was a fresh kill too.

The tall man reined in the black and white pinto beside the tower of red rocks. The sweat-foamed Ovaro came to a halt and shifted under him, shaking its mane. The midday sun blazed down, the heat rising in waves from the rocks and dry sand. The tall man's eyes narrowed as he squinted up at the blasting sun and at the slowly circling hawk. He instinctively touched the butt of the Henry rifle in the saddle scabbard. Trouble? His instincts told him yes. Honed to the sharpness of a fresh-stropped blade by years living in the wilds of the West, his sixth sense told him something was wrong in the vast landscape around him. He doffed his hat, mopped the sweat on his face, and glanced back at the Indian who accompanied him.

The Apache had spotted the hawk too and had come to a halt on his appaloosa. His hand rested on the hilt of the knife stuck in the buckskin sheath at his waist. His carmine face and muscular chest were glossy with sweat, his keen black eyes silent with a question.

Skye Fargo nodded at Akando silently, then glanced out at the horizon. In the distance, across a baked salt flat, a cloud of dust hid the party of riders they'd been following for three days. Not on purpose. He and Akando had met up by accident on the trail deep in Mexico. The Apache had been heading northward back to his tribe, and Fargo had business in Los Ricos. Riding through El Diablo with a friend was a helluva lot better than alone.

As they rode north, they had come on the trail of five riders going the same direction through El Diablo. The first night, while Akando guarded their two horses, Fargo had crept up on the strangers' camp to spy them out. There were four men and a woman—a young and beautiful woman with waist-length black hair and a voluptuous figure, Fargo had noted. The leader of the group seemed to be a short gentleman, dapper and imperious, with a silver-chased hat on his glistening black hair. The riders' clothing struck Fargo as vaguely foreign. More than that he couldn't learn. So he and Akando had followed along behind, staying far enough to the rear that the riders had no idea they were there.

Not many ventured into El Diablo. It was killing land. Anyone riding across it had to be desperate for something. Fargo had wondered many times during the past three days what had brought the party of five foreigners to El Diablo. But he had enough on his mind right now not to get into somebody else's business. If there was one thing you learned in El Diablo Country—it was to keep your distance.

Fargo's lake blue eyes followed the sudden flapping of a vulture above the mesquite that choked the dry riverbed to the west. What was the fresh kill out there? Likely a peccary, the bristly wild boar. Or else the remains of an armadillo flipped by a cougar. Probably nothing more than that. The riders they were following had swept right by without noticing. There were three hawks up in the sky now. Without a word Fargo turned the Ovaro off the trail and Akando followed.

They wound through the thick mesquite and palo verde until they spotted the dusty black flapping of four vultures. Fargo dismounted and walked over for a closer look. The story was as clear as words on paper to one who could read the signs. Fargo clapped his hands loudly and waved his arms. The vultures hopped away reluctantly, then flew to perches on nearby trees where they kept close watch on him.

Two Mexicans lay sprawled face up in the blistering sun, their faces disfigured by the vultures. They'd been dead about two hours. Dark bloody chests. Both shot dead center, close range. Powder burns—real close range. Their mouths gaped open, black blood staining what was left of their skin. Their tongues had been cut out.

"Gomez." Akando said. Even in the one word the Apache uttered, Fargo heard a note of wonder.

Yeah, the Gomez Gang. He hadn't heard about them for ten years. Jorge Gomez and his *bandidos* had rampaged through Mexico, robbing and pillaging. Mostly stagecoaches and shipments from Mexico City. Whenever anyone crossed them, the brutal gang cut out his tongue. Then Gomez and his band just seemed to disappear into El Diablo. Now here they were again.

The Apache turned and began circling the spot, reading the tracks in the dust. Fargo remained looking down at the bodies. They might be father and son. Their rough-woven serapes, battered sombreros, and callused hands marked them as poor men. The younger one wore a stained leather vest tooled with pictures of running horses and a pair of cheap spurs attached to his woven sandals, as if he had aspirations to become a wandering *vaquero,* hired by the rich *gringos* up north. But who were they?

Fargo knelt and quickly went through their pockets but found no clues. A silver glint at the neck of the older one caught Fargo's attention. He leaned over and yanked at the chain around the man's neck. A cloud of black flies swarmed, sounding angry in the heat. Dangling from the glittering chain was a piece of carved turquoise in the shape of a turtle. He'd show it around at Los Ricos. Maybe somebody would recognize it and know who the men were.

As Fargo moved away from the bodies, the vultures flew down. In the dust all around, the tracks were confusing. Cattle. Horses. Even a mule. Akando stepped out of the mesquite and wordlessly motioned him to come look. There, hidden in the brush, were marks where horses had been tethered and where men had slept the night without a fire.

Suddenly Akando squatted down and peered at the ground. Fargo leaned over him.

"Strange mark," Akando said, pointing. "Striped hoof."

"Some kind of marked horseshoe," Fargo said, examining the track. "A horseshoe scored across the bottom. I've never seen anything like it."

"They came from hills," Akando said, pointing west to the low, bare mounds, "and went back that way too." And they'd driven off the cattle that the two Mexicans had been herding. The Gomez Gang or whoever had killed the men was many miles away by now.

They rose and scoured the area again, but could find nothing else of use. As they mounted, Fargo thought of the five riders up ahead. The dust cloud was barely visible on the horizon now since the riders had got far ahead of them while they had stopped to search the gully.

"Let's pull in closer to 'em," Fargo said as they set off through the brush. Akando touched his moccasined heels to the sides of his appaloosa, and the horse sprang into a gallop. The Ovaro bounded forward. Fargo felt a sudden concern for the foreigners, especially for the woman. If Jorge Gomez and his *bandidos* were still lurking around, there was bound to be another ambush. Of course, the Gomez Gang was now driving the few stolen cattle and horses—something puzzled Fargo about that. Gomez had been famous for intercepting gold shipments, lifting jewels off wealthy lady travelers, and carrying away safes of cash from the rich ranchers. A few head of cattle from two poor Mexicans didn't seem like Gomez's style. Still, their tongues had been cut out. Who else would have done that?

The Ovaro and appaloosa kept an easy pace as they galloped down the hard-packed and curving streambed until they came to a rocky area. Fargo led them through up through the brush and out of the wash. At the edge of the cracked salt flat, Fargo paused for a moment.

Before them the white cracked land glittered in the broiling sun. On the far side, the dust cloud that had hidden the five riders before was now completely gone, dissipated among the jagged teeth of red rock that rimmed the flat. And that worried him. If they galloped straight across the glaring expanse, it would make them completely visible to anyone within fifteen miles, and they would come up to the towering red rocks utterly exposed. He and Akando could outride or outshoot anybody. But there was no telling what lay ahead. Fargo's eyes traced a path along the eastern edge of the flat, along a string of low red mesas. Riding at the foot of them would make their dust plume less visible, he decided. He nodded toward the east.

"Good," Akando agreed as he loosened the rifle in his saddle. They rode fast now, the horses pulling hard, in a lather, making a wide arc along the broken mesas. A few miles later, they approached the edge of the flat and slowed to a walk as they rode in among the tall red rocks. Fargo didn't like the feel of the place—too many places somebody could be hiding. He glanced back at Akando and saw his eyes alert, his body tensed, listening. It was impossible to see far ahead. Fargo spotted the tracks of the five riders, and they began to follow, winding up a gentle grade.

They had not gone far when the pop of gunfire broke out ahead of them and a woman screamed. They galloped forward as the sound of gunfire grew nearer. Fargo's Colt was in his hand, its silver barrel flashing in the sun. Suddenly, he heard men shouting and the gunfire redoubled.

The rocks ended abruptly, and Fargo saw in the clearing ahead the rising smoke of the battle. He reined in, and in a moment his eyes took in everything, the five riders pinned down in a circle of rocks, their horses scattered in terror as lead flew through the air. There were men hiding in the rocks around the clearing. He watched the rising of the gunsmoke. Two. Three, no, four men. He dismounted and, with one look, told Akando they'd split up. Running fast and low, keeping the rocks between himself and the ambushers, he dashed from cover to cover, making his way up the slope until he spotted one of the men, a scrawny-looking fellow hunched down behind a rock, popping up from time to time to take a shot at the five down below.

Fargo moved forward slowly until he had a clear shot, then raised his Colt and fired. The bullet caught the man in the back. He jerked forward and tumbled over. Fargo heard a shout and then more gunfire from across the clearing and knew Akando had found another of them.

Suddenly, a bullet whined by Fargo, grazing his cheek and shattering the rock behind him. There was a sudden scramble in the rocks above, and Fargo saw one of the ambushers, a small, skinny man dressed in peasant clothes, hightailing it up the slope, probably heading for his horse. Fargo ran after him through the rocks until he came into sight, untethering his horse.

"Halt," Fargo called out, cocking his pistol. The figure turned and Fargo saw his face. It was a young Mexican boy. And scared. He raised a rifle, but it was shaking in his hand.

The boy froze, panic on his face. Then he jerked the bridle of his horse and started to swing onto it. Fargo took slow aim and winged the kid. He dropped his rifle and stumbled, then pitched to the ground. Fargo sprang forward and hauled the kid up by his shirt. There was still the pop of gunfire on the far side and Fargo knew Akando was trying to get the last of the four.

"Who the hell are you?" Fargo said, shaking him. The boy was no more than twelve, and his frightened eyes were ringed with dark circles. One thing for sure. The kid hadn't come on his own. "Who sent you here?"

The kid swore in Spanish and Fargo shook him again.

"Answer me. Who sent you here?"

"Ramirez," the kid panted, holding his bleeding shoulder. "The Generalissimo." He looked up at Fargo as if that explained everything. Fargo had heard of Vito Ramirez, famous in all of Mexico as an Indian fighter and a powerful politician.

"You're not part of the army," Fargo said, disbelieving.

"No. Ramirez." The boy spat in the dust at the name. "We find him. Me and my brothers. Over there." The boy jerked his head in the direction of the riders. Fargo had seen pictures of the Generalissimo, and he knew the kid was mistaken. The famous Ramirez was not with the five riders.

"You were trying to *ambush* Generalissimo Ramirez?" Fargo said. The boy nodded his head vigorously.

The gunfire had ceased, and there were voices calling from down below. Fargo heard footsteps and turned to see the short gentleman he'd spotted before heading toward him, a pearl-handled revolver in his hands. The sunlight sparkled on his silver-chased hat. His boots were of the best tooled leather. His face, narrow and long, had a strong jaw and prominent cheekbones. Under his heavy lids, the dark brown eyes looked at everything coolly as if weary, bored. One of the other men, a big fellow in black, followed with a rifle.

"Who are you?" the gentleman asked in Spanish, his revolver covering both of them.

"I just saved your necks," Fargo snapped back. The short gentleman smiled very slowly, his black brows arched imperiously.

"So you did," he said slowly. "I am Prospero Aznar, Count of Seville." He drew himself up importantly and glared at Fargo. So, he'd been right, Fargo thought. The riders were foreigners, all the way from Spain.

"And this is my man, Manrique." The count waved in the direction of the big man standing warily nearby. "And who is this, this peasant?" The count looked disdainfully at the boy.

"He thinks you're Generalissimo Vito Ramirez," Fargo said.

Prospero Aznar laughed heartily at this and so did the big fellow Manrique. The kid held his bleeding shoulder and glanced from one to the other, his eyes dark and miserable.

"Why were you looking for Ramirez?" Fargo asked the kid again.

"Because of . . . Because Gomez," the kid said. "Los Ricos. The Generalissimo, he is making us—"

The shot took Fargo by surprise, the bullet exploding from Prospero Aznar's pistol, catching the kid in the belly. A look of surprise passed over the young kid's face in an instant, and then he slumped to the ground. A trickle of blood darkened the gritty sand. The puff of gunsmoke blew away in the breeze.

"What the hell?" Fargo swore. He took a menacing step toward Aznar. "What the hell did you do that for?"

"Peasant," Aznar said. He pulled a silk handkerchief from his pocket and buffed the barrel of his pistol. The count's bodyguard grunted in approval. "It is a waste of time to listen to peasants talk."

Fargo felt a tide of rage rise in him, and he lashed out, driving a fist into Prospero Aznar's smooth jaw. The count stumbled backward, and with a yell Manrique sprang forward and grabbed Fargo by the neck. They went down and rolled in the dust, over and over, struggling for a grip. The big fellow was strong, his arms like iron.

Fargo rolled on top of him and landed a right square in Manrique's belly, then a left uppercut that threw his head back against the hard ground. But Manrique rallied, swore in Spanish, and suddenly began pummeling with his fists, a pounding flurry that caught Fargo in the belly, the jaw, the chest. The big man's fists were huge, like meaty clubs, and he knew how to use them too. They pulled apart and got wearily to their feet, facing off.

Manrique's eyes were emotionless, empty, intent on his prey. Fargo became aware of others approaching as the big man closed in. He didn't like the idea of duking it out with the rest of Aznar's company surrounding him. It was time to get this over with. Summoning all his strength, Fargo drew back his powerful arm and delivered a forceful blow that caught Manrique square on the jaw, almost snapping his head around. The big man staggered backward with the force of the impact, blinking his eyes. His knees weakened and he suddenly went down, his eyes rolling backward in his head.

Fargo pulled the bandanna from around his neck and mopped his face. The others had come up to surround them.

"Oh, Father! Are you all right?"

Fargo turned to see the woman running toward the count. She was even more exquisite up close. She was short, like her father, her figure extravagantly rounded with a tiny waist and high-mounded breasts that poured over the top of her low-cut black dress. Her waist-length hair gleamed like black fire in the sunlight. She glanced at Fargo, and he felt immediately that there was something catlike in her face with its quiet, dark eyes that seemed to see everything, wide cheekbones, and pointed chin. Then she smiled at him and seemed transformed into a kittenish young woman.

Following her like a panting bloodhound was a redheaded pale fellow in plaid pants and shirt. In his hand he carried a forked stick. Serena reached her father and wrapped her arms around him as he patted her on the shoulder.

"I am fine, Serena. We are safe now." The count glanced over at Fargo, as if he wanted to apologize. "*Señor* . . ."

"Fargo. Skye Fargo."

"Ah, *Señor* Fargo. My apologies for the behavior of my man, Manrique. He can be so hot-headed." The count offered his hand. Serena was watching his closely, and he felt her eyes travel over his hard-muscled body, his powerful chest.

Fargo nodded but refused to shake with the count, still burned up that Aznar had shot the kid before he'd had a chance to find out what this was all about. It was as if the count wanted to hush up the kid before he could talk. The redheaded fellow curiously poked the dead peasant boy with one end of his stick.

"The kid was looking for Generalissimo Ramirez," Fargo muttered, almost to himself. The redhead looked up at the words.

"Ramirez!" he exclaimed. "Why, ain't that a coincidence? We was just waiting for the Generalissimo to show up here. By the by, I'm Hagan Crowley. Seeker and finder."

Fargo shook the man's hand, his thoughts whirling. So,

Prospero Aznar had come here to rendezvous with Ramirez. The kid hadn't been far wrong.

"Seeker and finder of what?" Fargo asked Crowley. Hagan Crowley raised his forked stick.

"Water in the desert," Crowley said grandly, waving his stick in the air. "I can find silver in streams. Husbands who have run away. Kidnapped children. Lost horses. Missing cattle. Buried treasure—"

"That's enough," the count snapped. He turned to Fargo and said in a different tone of voice, "Tell me, *Señor* Fargo, what brings you to El Diablo?"

"Just passing through," Fargo replied shortly. He had business in El Diablo, all right, he thought. But he'd keep it to himself.

"Where are you heading?"

"A little place you've never heard of," the count said, smiling.

"It's a town called Los Ricos," Serena said, and her eyes glittered with some emotion he could not identify. "It means *the rich ones*. It is supposed to be a very pretty town." She glanced at her father. "Maybe we will build a castle there."

He smiled indulgently at her.

"Los Ricos," Fargo said slowly. "Nope, never heard of it," he lied.

Yeah, his instinct had been right to keep his mouth shut about his destination. Fargo turned about abruptly and went to fetch the kid's horse while his thoughts whirled. The message had come by word of mouth a week before when he and Akando had been running down some rustlers and rounding up horses for a drive back over the border. One afternoon a monk named Father Salvatore had appeared on a donkey looking for him.

"*Señor* Fargo, I think you are the only one who can help," Father Salvatore had told him. "In the town of Los Ricos I met a man named Gregorio. As soon as he saw me arrive, he told me to get out, that the whole town was doomed to die."

"And you believed him?" Fargo asked.

"He was not crazy," Father Salvatore answered thoughtfully. "He was nervous and kept looking over his shoulder. The next day we were going to meet at the cantina, and he promised to tell me everything he suspected. Why he was afraid. But the next day he was gone. And he never came back." Father Salvatore glanced up at Fargo then. "I know what you are thinking," he continued. "But I cannot explain. I saw something wrong in the town. The people, they were afraid. Something terrible will happen there, but I do not know what. Everybody knows the reputation of the Trailsman, the man who can find the tracks that others do not see. There is some invisible evil in this town." Father Salvatore opened the leather pouch that hung at his rope belt. "I know in my heart there is trouble there in Los Ricos. I will give you money, pay your fee."

"Keep your *pesos* for the poor," Fargo had answered. "I'll go down to Los Ricos." If there was trouble brewing down there, he had thought at the time, it was sure to find him. It always did.

Now, as he led the boy's horse back toward the waiting group, he was sure he'd stumbled right into the middle of it.

Count Aznar sent his three men out to round up the horses. Fargo searched the rocks and found one other of the ambushers, who had obviously been shot by Akando. He turned the body face up and saw that it was another kid, about the same age as the one shot by the count. Fargo swore to himself. What were these boys up to? He set out to find the fourth one, then spotted some blood stains on the rocks, droplets that led up to where a horse had been tethered. Then tracks leading away. Fargo followed them for a short distance and saw them joined by another horse.

So that's where Akando had gone. He'd probably shot the first ambusher, just as Fargo had, without noticing it was a kid. Then he'd winged the second and followed him as he escaped to see where he went. Fargo returned to the group which had assembled near the low rock circle. The big one named Manrique had come around and was saddling up. He glared at Fargo. A deep red marked Manrique's jaw, and it would turn into a helluva bruise.

Fargo took a swig from his canteen, then poured water into his hat and let the Ovaro drink.

"You are a very brave man," Serena said, sidling up to him. Her shoulders were bare and lovely in the lowering sun, and the firm mounds of her breasts had a deep shadow between them. She smiled, kittenish again. "You are riding alone?"

Fargo felt suddenly on guard. He didn't want to mention Akando. The less he told them, he decided, the better. He didn't trust the count and his men, or even Serena. They were all up to something. But what?

"I guess you could say that every man rides alone in El Diablo," Fargo said lightly.

"But what is your business?" she said. "It must be very interesting." She reached out one finger and lightly traced the line of buttons down the front of his shirt, her eyes on his chest. Her touch was electric, and he wanted to seize her, bend her soft curves to his will. "So strong." Her hand dropped to the butt of his Colt, which she touched lightly, then put her finger to her lips. "And I think, yes, I think this gun has killed many, many men." She glanced into his face again as if trying to read him. That dark gleam behind her eyes again. There it was. "Yes, I think it must be very interesting business that brings you to El Diablo."

"Going from one place to the next," he said. She was like a snake, a cougar, a cat.

"Well, *Señor,*" the count said, preparing to mount. "It has been a pleasure running into you. Thank you for your assistance in driving off these attacking peasants. And now, which way are you heading?"

"I think I'm going to tag along up to Los Ricos," Fargo said lightly. "Never been that way before. Sounds like an interesting place."

"But . . . but—" Hagan Crowley looked panicked, his pale face reddening.

"Shut up," the count snapped, his face betraying an emotion, like a wave of anger. Then it passed as he controlled his expression by putting on a tight smile.

"Wonderful," he said, turning his horse about.

"Wonderful," Serena repeated with her enigmatic smile. She swung onto her horse, a spirited stallion. From her seat and the way she held the reins, Fargo could tell she was an expert rider. They started off, with Manrique in the lead. Fargo brought up the rear following Serena. She looked back from time to time, her long hair blowing in the wind like a wild horse's tail.

She was damned fine-looking, Fargo thought. But something told him she had a black heart. Just like her father. Yeah, he'd stumbled right into it this time. Trouble had its way of finding him. And he was sure there was even more trouble ahead, up in the town of Los Ricos.